Benjamin Gastineau, Edmond Dubourg

Voltaire in exile

His life and works in France and abroad

Benjamin Gastineau, Edmond Dubourg

Voltaire in exile
His life and works in France and abroad

ISBN/EAN: 9783337197940

Printed in Europe, USA, Canada, Australia, Japan

Cover: Foto ©Raphael Reischuk / pixelio.de

More available books at **www.hansebooks.com**

CENTENARY OF VOLTAIRE.

VOLTAIRE IN EXILE:

HIS LIFE AND WORKS IN FRANCE AND ABROAD

(ENGLAND, HOLLAND, BELGIUM, PRUSSIA, SWITZERLAND),

WITH

UNPUBLISHED LETTERS OF VOLTAIRE AND MME. DU CHATELET.

BY BENJAMIN GASTINEAU.

Translated with the author's approval by Messrs. F. Vogeli and
Edmond Dubourg.

D. M. BENNETT,
LIBERAL AND SCIENTIFIC PUBLISHING HOUSE,
141 EIGHTH ST., NEW YORK.

TABLE OF CONTENTS.

	PAGE.
Translators' Preface,	iii
Centenary of Voltaire,	3
Introduction,	9
Chap. I.—Voltaire's Youth,	17
Chap. II.—Voltaire in Exile,	28
Chap. III.—Return to Paris,	35
Chap. IV.—Voltaire in Brussels,	42
Chap. V.—Voltaire and J. J. Rousseau,	46
Chap. VI.—Voltaire and the Abbe Prevost,	53
Chap. VII.—Voltaire and Frederick the Great,	60
Chap. VIII.—Voltaire and Pope Benedict XIV.,	66
Chap. IX.—Voltaire in Berlin,	74
Chap. X.—Third Return to Paris.	80
Chap. XI.—Leaves Again for Berlin,	85
Chap. XII.—Coolness Between Him and Frederick,	90
Chap. XIII.—Life in Switzerland,	97
Chap. XIV.—Voltaire at Ferney,	115
Chap. XV.—Improves a Town, Builds a Church, and Fights the Jesuits,	122
Chap. XVI.—Defends the Victims of Religious Hatred and Persecution,	129
Chap. XVII.—Voltaire and Catharine II.,	135
Chap. XVIII.—Triumphant Return to Paris,	143
Chap. XIX.—The Work of Voltaire,	155
Chap. XX.—Voltaire's Propagandism,	167
Chap. XXI.—Philosophical System,	179
Chap. XXII.—The Enemies of Voltaire,	201
Chap. XXIII.—Voltaire as a Poet and Dramatic Author,	209
Appendix.—Unpublished Letters,	224

TRANSLATOR'S PREFACE.

A desire on the occasion of the centenary of Voltaire to pay a tribute to his memory, and a genuine admiration for that master mind of the eighteenth century, have prompted the author of *Voltaire in Exile* to the writing of these pages. The loyal feelings of the biographer, so often apt in imparting a bias to his appreciation and sketching of traits, have not been permitted in this case, however, so to tint the lineaments of the philosopher's character that, the defects which stamped him as a man being passed or glossed over, his glowing qualities, unimpeded, might make him appear the greater hero. That Voltaire possessed faults cannot be denied. Yet it redounds to his praise that his faults were rather those of the age than of the man. As much could not be said of many men of less genius and of other ages.

Aside from the unpardonable sin of blasphemy and the use of every conceivable means to foil his enemies and cover them with well-merited ridicule, there stands against Voltaire but one accusation of weight. With regard to his alleged use of unscrupulous means in the increase of his wealth, the simple facts, as given in the course of this work, are sufficient to show how absurd were the attacks of that lilliputian church rabble so ready, nevertheless, to fawn upon every monopolist or stock speculator who will but donate a tithe of his ill-gotten gains to the " houses

of God." But there remains against the great icon-
oclast the charge of holding broad notions concerning the relations of the sexes and transgressing the
social laws which govern them.

This book is meant to be a faithful history of Voltaire, a picture as unbiased and perfect as it could be
photographed, so to speak, by the hand of an admiring
but conscientious artist. The phases and evolutions
of the great man's character are left to be observed
through the continuous panorama of his eventful and
active life. We are first introduced to a young man
in whom genius with all its concomitant temptations
is already revealing itself to a nature which, with its
inborn Epicurean tastes, was easily led through the
influence of the surrounding and general Christian
licentiousness into a participation in its dissolute
ways. In his day "the lover, *l'ami intime*," to use
the words of a writer in the Argosy, " was an indis-
pensable part of every fine lady's household. It is
true that both the fair dames and their cavaliers
were frequently seen at mass and all sorts of religious ceremonies, but they went back to the *salon* to
flirt and make love quite as briskly as ever." Voltaire simply lived as men of the world in his time
lived. Therein lies his only weakness, that, high as
he towered in heart and intellect above the Christian herd among which he lived, he did not rise
above them in social morality.

But, if having admitted and regretting this (for an
apostle of the truth should be above reproach, even
from those who, in every respect, are beneath him),
we now turn to the work of the philosopher, we are
seized with such admiration that the weaknesses of
the man are forgotten and entirely swallowed up in

his brilliancy, greatness, and philanthropy. When we behold him the equal of kings and protector of the weak, armed with the sword of philosophy and truth opposing, almost single-handed, the combined and exasperated forces of superstition, cant, ecclesiastical falsehood, and priestly despotism; lacerating them with his terrible sarcasm, and scattering them in every direction; then view the humanitarian, ever watchful and ready to step forward and champion the cause of the oppressed, giving them his time, his genius, his money, his hospitality; and, lastly, see the public benefactor at Ferney, where the practical bearings and results of his life-long principles are illustrated in his becoming the author of the prosperity and happiness of a hitherto stagnant community, we grant him not admiration alone, but also the profound veneration which true goodness, allied to genius, must ever command. We can then look down with tranquil contempt upon the tartuffian crowd that would blot his fame to stifle his ideas, and cover him with the slime of their calumny and abuse to prevent his genius from lighting up the philosophical world.

Therefore let faithful biographies of Voltaire multiply without fearing to reproduce every feature of his wonderful character. This greatest of the champions of Freethought, whom his enemies have belied to the point of stamping with the universal reputation of an Atheist the man who, right or wrong, persistently declared his belief in a supreme being, needs but to become known, such as he really was, to also become endeared, in spite of his faults, to all who, whatever their philosophical creed, have a love for truth, justice, and liberty.

VOLTAIRE'S CENTENARY.

I regretfully leave Voltaire, after having passed three months with him.

I had long been an admirer of the great philosopher who was the leader of Freethought in the eighteenth century. By living in his intimacy, by scrutinizing his life and work, I have become his friend; and, if they are not already so, I am convinced my readers will become his friends as I have, after perusing this work, where I have endeavored to seize upon his encyclopedic genius, his mobile and multiple physiognomy.

How can we but become the liegemen, the intellectual associates of Voltaire, when we see him consecrate all his life to the cause of civilization, of truth, of the liberty of conscience and thought; when we behold his struggle in France against political despotism and religious obscurantism; when we accompany him to his retreats in exile where he courageously takes up again his interrupted work and freely publishes his productions?

It is with an inexpressible joy that we follow the steps of this scout of the human army, of this pioneer making deep gaps in the forest of prejudices, bringing new light at each one of his stages, and that we behold the victory of the mind upon human errors and folly.

Voltaire will be the great figure, eternally be-
witching and attractive, of the eighteenth century.
He fought the good fight, and carried the victory.
He established tolerance, liberated conscience from
its oppressions, affranchised thought from its chains,
wrote the preface of the Civil Code and of the Revolution of '89, destroyed the barbarous legislations,
superannuated customs, old traditions, prejudices,
all the obstacles, all the impediments which hindered
the march of civilization. He has been the martial
champion of the mind, the hero of free humanity.

His country *embastilled* him, persecuted him, threw
his books to the flames, exiled him nearly all his life.

Voltaire burst into laughter in the face of that
race of *arlequins anthropophages*, as he called the
proscribers of Louis XV.; he made sport of *censure*
and *lettre de cachet*. He pursued his crusade of
Freethought in all his places of retreat; in England,
Holland, Belgium, Prussia, Switzerland; where, con-
nected with the eminent minds of those lands, he
founded the public opinion of Europe, which, through
his propaganda, became an irresistible power against
all public iniquities, against all infractions of the
rights and liberty of man.

Voltaire sums up in himself all the eighteenth
century, with its genius sparkling like champagne
in its bowl, its absolute separation from a shameful
and retrograde past, its vigorous flight towards
progress, towards a new state of civilization disen-
gaged from all that is base, servile, and obscure.

By this resplendent light projected by the age of
Voltaire, how deformed and shrunken appears the
ancient slave trembling before priest and master!
But wait until the philosophers have restored to the

mutilated being of the Middle Ages his mind, his soul, his will, his intellectual and moral power—until they have delivered him from the jail of the seventeenth century; and you will see the poor man renewed and transformed by the Promethei of the Encyclopedia; you shall see him walk erect and firm in his strength and liberty. Ah, masters! you throw Voltaire in the Bastille, and you proscribe him. His vengeance shall be exemplary. He will bring out with him from his dungeon the enchained generations, and he will return, in spite of you, triumphant to those lands from which you had believed him forever banished.

There is not in the world a more marvelous, more attractive spectacle, one better demonstrating the power of a luminous and sagacious mind, than the polemic of Voltaire against the birds of prey and the men of darkness of his time. What a vivacious and high intelligence, what ardor of conviction, what good sense, what acumen in critique, one of his creations! What lucidity of conception and expression! What a pliant and fine blade! "His prose is a sword," says Nisard; "it sparkles, it whizzes, it thrusts forward, it slays!"

A knight armed from head to foot, brilliant and sprightly combatant, how well he strikes at the fault of the cuirass, the leviathans, the mastodons of the old regime! He harasses them ceaselessly with his barbed arrows; he smites oppression in all its forms, snatching away the mask of religious hypocrisy, stigmatizing superstition, lifting up man bent under secular servitudes, extricating his mind from the silly errors, from the chimeras, that dwarf him, by saying to him:

"Cultivate thy garden and thy brain; cleanse
them from the old sediments, from the calcareous
deposits and the detritus of the past. Burn the
brambles and parasite herbs; destroy the noxious
insects; let the mattock pass everywhere. Thou art
king, lord, and master at home. Draw straight and
see clearly. Do not fall in the rut of Utopia; do not
lose thyself in the abyss of dreams. No power has
the right to weigh down upon thee, to violate thy
intellectual property and material good. Throw to
the garret all the worm-eaten cabalistic books, the
old Bibles and old codes, and find thy evangel in
thy reason; thy law and rule in thy conscience."

The universality, the prodigious intellectual activity of Voltaire allowed him to span all problems;
his quick and sensitive genius, his straightforward
sense, carry him wherever there is a truth useful to
bring forth, an error to confound, an injustice to
disgrace.

He is the support, the spur, of that valiant crew
of encyclopedists who forged the conception of the
new society; he encourages them, animates them
with his noble ardor, with his hatred against the
Catholic denomination, by preaching through example and ceaselessly exclaiming, "Crush the wretch!"

We find the generous and beneficent hand of Voltaire in the salient facts of the eighteenth century.
He touches everything; nothing for him lacks interest. He was not only a profound thinker, philosopher, historian, man of letters, poet, dramatic author,
popularizer of science, but he was, besides, "the
hero and the man of action of right," as a Belgian
deputy, M. Belgé, has said in a lecture. Possessing
to a supreme degree the love of humanity, he con-

siders all wrong done to others as if it were personal
to him.　He leaps with indignation on witnessing a
public iniquity.　He constitutes himself the juris-
consult, the high judge of his time.　The victims of
fanaticism, persecution, and judiciary errors come
to him.　He welcomes them, he throws wide open
to them the doors of his house at Ferney, takes in
hand their grievances, becomes their eloquent defender, and succeeds in snatching them away from
the fury of the Catholic tribunals.

The obscurantist and Jesuitic pack threw itself,
howling and furious, upon this knight of Freethought; but, smiling in the thick of the *melee*, Voltaire marked with his eagle claw the enemies of reason, and devoted the spirits of darkness and the
Tartuffes to the immortality of ridicule.

After fifty years in the philosophical arena, fifty
years of conflicts constantly renewed without ex-
hausting the athlete, Voltaire remains at last master
of the field.　He triumphs over the retrograde elements of the old society.　All the despotisms, tem-
poral and spiritual, have Voltairian shot in their
wing.　They have lost their assurance, their audaci-
ty; they drag themselves and gasp, mortally wounded by the skillful hunter.

Is it to be wondered at that, a hundred years after
the Iliad, after the great battle of the eighteenth
century, "the deceiving spirits, teaching lies and
hypocrisy," to borrow from de Sainte-Aldegonde,
"the 'black band,' Jesuitic and despotic, shudders
at the very name of Voltaire, of that Satan of the
mind, as he is qualified by one of the greatest cori-
phæi of the Church, Joseph de Maistre, who expressed the wish to see a statue raised to him by the

hand of the executioner, and who, in an avowal devoid of artifice, exclaimed, "Ah! what harm Voltaire has done us!"

The labors of Hercules are but child's play by the side of Voltaire's.

His encyclopedic mind has shone upon all the branches of human knowledge. Philosophy, politics, legislation, morals—there is not one social element which he has not touched, shed light upon, and reformed.

Let the Revolution come; it will only have to bind up in sheaves the grain of the Voltairian harvest, to countersign and decree the ideas of Voltaire. And in '89 Condorcet will be able to say with truth, "Voltaire a fait tout ce que nous voyons!" ("Voltaire is the author of all that we see!")

All the sons of Freethought unite to-day in the glorification of Voltaire, in his centenary, honoring in him the luminous genius that has more and better than any other honored and served humanity, the highest expression and the most illustrious representative of European civilization.

INTRODUCTION.

Voltaire, that Wandering Jew of intelligence and Freethought in the eighteenth century, does not belong only to France, from which he was forced to flee nearly all his life, but to all the lands where he sought refuge to save himself from the chronic intolerance of his fellow-countrymen—to the Netherlands, to England, to Prussia, and to Switzerland. At these hearths he found established, radiant and powerful, the political and religious liberties which he strove to take back and to make triumph in his native land.

Voltaire forged his genius upon the hard anvil and at the rough school of exile. To this he owed his fame. Had he remained at the French court he would have been but a mere witling, a rare bird in the golden cage of Versailles.

In London, in Amsterdam, Berlin, Brussels, Geneva, Voltaire found the lever of Archimedes, the fulcrum that was necessary to him in lifting the world and enlightening it. It was abroad that he was able to fight openly, to write freely, to publish his works, to propagate his ideas, without risking, as it had happened to him in France, to be bastinadoed, *embastilled*, and to see his books burnt by the hand of the executioner.

The funeral march of the Wandering Jews of Freethought begins with the revocation of the edict of Nantes and the dragonnades of the Cevennes,

under King Louis XIV, in his second childhood, that
nec pluribus impar which terminated his existence
by the fistula and Madame de Maintenon. The Huguenots deserted *en masse* from Catholic France,
carrying away with them their gold, their art, their
science, their industry, to take them to the Protestant nations, by whom they were received with open
arms.

After the religionists of the seventeenth come the
Freethinkers of the eighteenth, lastly the politicians
of the nineteenth century.

It is the great and painful pilgrimage of Liberty
in mourning.

Belgium, Holland, England, Switzerland, Germany, behold coming to them legions of fugitives,
seeking a new hearth, a new fatherland.

In the seventeenth century the Huguenots leaving
France merely passed through Catholic Belgium.

The United Provinces received no less than 55,000
French Protestant refugees; England received 100,-
000 of them, who endowed her with all the precious
industries of France.

Migrations, whether voluntary or forced, have
two consequences: impoverishment of the countries
they abandon, increase of vitality and riches for the
regions where they land and which they fructify, as
the periodical overflows of the Nile fecundate the
lands they water.

Emigration alone has created the formidable
power of the United States. The emigration of the
Old World has brought forth and enriched the
New.

But refugees do not only carry material benefits
to the countries that receive them ; they carry to

them, besides, the precious tributes of their science, of their art, of their intelligence. In return they receive a strength, a development, an increase of light, as is proven by Voltaire, exiled in the Netherlands, in England, and in Switzerland.

Before reaching Voltaire, it will be useful to say something of the French exiles who preceded him in his first places of refuge, Belgium and Holland.

In the seventeenth century we see in Belgium an illustrious refugee, Antoine Arnauld, the Hercules of Jansenism, the director of the nuns and pensionnaires of Port Royal.

Denounced by the Jesuits, accused of conspiracy and intrigue against the State, Arnauld crossed the frontier. It was natural for him to seek refuge in the country where Jansenius had been bishop and professor of Holy Scriptures. After having resided at Mons, Arnauld settled permanently at Brussels, for he died there in the course of the year 1694. He was interred under the flagstones of Catherine Church, and his heart was taken to Port Royal des Champs.

Bayle, the illustrious author of the *Dictionaire Historique et Critique*, who, in his professor's chair at Sedan and in his writings, had courageously fought the religious intolerance of Louis XIV, was also compelled to take the road of exile. Before reaching Amsterdam, there to edit his *Nouvelles de la Republique des Lettres*, he stopped in Brussels, but he left there no appreciable trace of his abode.

The famous comic poet, Regnard, also remained a short while in Brussels in the course of 1681, and there found time to grasp the subject of the best comedy in his repertory. Here are the facts:

At Rome, with the general of the Jesuits, suddenly died an old gentleman of Franche Comté, the lord d' Ancier.

· That abrupt and unlucky decease had completely upset the plans of the good Jesuit fathers, who had lodged and fondled our Franche Comté gentleman thus well only to have him make his will in favor of their order and to inherit all his goods, according to their custom. But such a small affair did not perplex our Jesuits ; they concealed the nobleman's death and sought a *Sosia* who could make the will in his room and stead.

One of the members of the company had known in Franche Comté a farmer of M. d' Ancier, Denis Euvrard by name, who had the same looks and the same tone of voice as his lord. He was despatched to that tenant, and, through promises of money, succeeded in bringing him to Rome. There he was told that his former lord had just died *ab intestat*, but not, however, before having had time to declare to the Jesuits that he had bequeathed an important farm to Denis Euvrard, and the remainder of his property to the reverend fathers.

· The general-of the order urged Denis in the name of heaven to carry out the desire of his defunct master by playing the part of the lord of Ancier on his bed of agony, by bringing him to life again for a few hours.

And so there was Denis Euvrard, our pseudo dying man, stretched upon his bed, with a nightcap down over his eyes, dictating his will—the will of the lord of Ancier—before witnesses and attorneys; but Denis, like the roguish countryman he was, instead of simply allotting to himself a farm, as it had been agreed with the Jesuits, added thereto appurtenances—*item* a mill, *item* a meadow, *item* a woodpatch, *item* some cattle, *item* rents.

At every item of Denis' the Jesuits, seeing themselves fooled, grew pale and foamed with rage. They were caught like foxes in their own trap.

At last the mock dying lord deigned to leave a part of the heritage to the reverend fathers, who were furious at thus seeing themselves defrauded of the best portion of the cake, yet were obliged to hold their peace in order to save the rest.

On the day after that sacrilegious farce the true d' Ancier was buried, and Denis Euvrard returned to his hearth, rich, in good health, and delighted at having thus hoodwinked the reverend Jesuit fathers.

Years passed away, and the mimic of death, playing seriously this time the part of a dying man, acknowledged his fraud and revealed the source of his fortune to his confessor. This priest, who was gallican, divulged the will scene concocted by the Jesuits. The natural heirs of M. d' Ancier then attacked the testament. They gained their cause twice, at Besançon and Dole; but the Jesuits, having carried the suit to the Supreme Court of Brussels (Franche Comté, subdued by Spain, depended at that time upon the Flemish government), this tribunal maintained the Jesuits in their right of mortmain upon what property of d' Ancier was held by them.

This suit had not been ended very long before Regnard was in Brussels. It was yet talked and laughed about. Thus it was that the reverend fathers furnished Regnard the idea of his excellent

comedy of the *Légataire Universel.* We see the
Jesuits are yet of some use, since they have so happily inspired Moliere in *Tartuffe,* Beaumarchais in
the Marriage de Figaro, and Regnard in the *Légataire.*

We are in the eighteenth century, so justly called
the age of Voltaire. At last the dazzling dawn of
Freethought has arrived. It arises, shedding a tor-
rent of light upon its obscure blasphemers, according
to the expression of Lefranc de Pompignan.

What an age! And how aptly has Hegel named
it the *age of intelligence.* Such intellectual radia-
tion; such philosophical magnetism; such buoyancy,
and such *salons!* All the literary minds participate
in the great work of the emancipation of the human
mind. The most brilliant names of the aristocracy
and of the rising *bourgeois,* of the nobility and the
finance, actively coöperate in the work of renovation,
for the eighteenth century was a new manner of
viewing all things, an intellectual and moral revolution. Lastly, the most noble women and the women
the most noble—Mesdames du Chatelet, du Deffant,
d'Tencin, de L'Espinasse, d'Houdetot, Geoffrin, Helvetius, d'Epinay, de Choiseul, de Grammout, de Lux-
embourg—I forget many more—these duchesses,
these marchionesses, these countesses, do not disdain
to be the Amazons of Freethought. At their houses
are held the philosophical assizes. Their parlors are
opened to the encyclopedists, to the philosophers,
discussing with them the great problems of human
destiny, bringing, as their part of the collaboration,
their graces and sparkling wit.

How precious that collaboration! and how much
it is to be regretted that the *bourgeois* of the nine-

teenth century have not seen fit to follow the example of their noble predecessors!

In the midst of that brilliant pleiad of encyclopedists and philosophical great ladies, vindicating the rights of Freethought, appears, like a knight in full armor, Voltaire, who exercised a prodigious influence upon his time, upon his age, of which he was the leader, as well as the highest intellectual expression.

Voltaire represented the tendencies of the minds of his period ; he stands for free conscience and typifies the virile ideas of that great eighteenth century, which Mr. Blaze de Bury has happily characterized as follows:

"In science, a spirit of free research; in literature, the free expansion of the true, of the human beautiful;" and we will add to that definition of M. Blaze. In the sphere of the philosophical, absolute reaction against Christianity, entire separation, antithesis of the Christian idea that makes human destiny to depend upon divine grace and intervention, whilst the philosophy of the eighteenth century—man is dependent only upon himself—upon the laws of his conscience and reason.

Christianity, as indeed do all religions, establishes the rights of God. The eighteenth century establishes the rights of man, so clearly formulated by the laws of the French Revolution, which was the product and the crowning of its philosophy. The eighteenth century is the legislator of the inevitable law of progress upon which we live to-day, and which vivifies us as our very blood.

Through the influence of Voltaire and of the encyclopedists, the period of Louis XV. was a complete revolution in thought, literature, and art.

On this point David Frederick Strauss has said, in one of his remarkable lectures upon Voltaire:

"The great work of the sixteenth century, the Reformation, is essentially the deed of the Germans; during the period of transition marked by the seventeenth century, whilst Germany was torn by civil struggle, Holland and England were establishing the foundations of modern politics and thought. In the eighteenth, Englishmen scattered in France, like Bolingbroke, Frenchmen visiting England, as Voltaire and Montesquieu, brought the spark of the new light which, thanks to the efforts of Voltaire, was to spring from France to beam upon the entire world, as the light of the age of vulgarization. If the French, and above all the Parisians, were the people elected to this intellectual priesthood, Voltaire was its high-priest; and we say with equal truth, In France alone the eighteenth century could find its literary representative; or in the eighteenth century alone could France produce the writer capable of reflecting within himself all her national qualities.

VOLTAIRE IN EXILE.

HIS LIFE AND WORK IN FRANCE AND IN FOREIGN
LANDS.

I.

Voltaire had a very stormy youth—ordinary par-
turition of great men.

A student in the college Louis-le-Grand, directed
by the Jesuits, to whom he was destined to give
such rude blows, he filled his teachers with admiration.

A celebrated Aspasia, who loved science, intelligence, and liberty as much as love, Ninon de L'Enclos,
was so much charmed with the keen intellect of the
young collegian that she desired to be his intellectual
godmother. She bequeathed him in her will two
thousand pistoles " for the purchase of books."

His classical studies were hardly terminated when
Voltaire abandoned himself to his poetical inspira-
tion. Quatrains and epigrams already circulated
around him. His father, M. Arouet, payer of fees
in the Chamber of Accounts, absolutely desiring to
cauterize the poetical mania of his son, and to prevent him from sacrificing to the muses, in order to
make him like himself a model notary, imagined
nothing better than to banish him to Holland, near
the Embassador of France, the Marquess of Châ-
teauneuf.

At Hague, in spite of the rigid supervision of the Marquess, the young Arouet lighted up the foggy sky of Holland with the sun of his youth. He began an amorous intrigue with Olympia Dunoyer, whom he surnamed Pimpette. The young girl was to that degree enamored with Arouet that she would come to see him in masculine disguise.

This affair did not suit the mother, Theresa Dunoyer, an intriguing woman, who aspired to wed Pimpette to some high personage. It seems that Cavalier, the hero of the Cévennes, was among the pretenders to the hand of Olympia.

To avoid a scandal, and being interested in managing Pimpette's mother, then director of the *Quintessence*, a magazine of clippings, of piquant anecdotes and flippant gossips, the Embassador interrupted the relations of the lovers by sending Voltaire back to his father, to whom he described him as incorrigible, incapable of being held in check, and a precocious rascal. He represented his amorous prank in the blackest colors in his missive, which he began thus:

"I have no more hope for your son. He is twice cracked: in love and a poet."

He called those things follies, the old diplomat!

Paraphrasing him, the good man Arouet dolefully said:

"I have for my sons two fools: the one in verse, the other in prose."

The "fool in prose" was the elder brother of Voltaire, who had become a Jansenist.

Voltaire returned to France by the way of Gand, whence he wrote to his Pimpette.

In 1716 he was banished to Sully-sur-Loire for

having lampooned the doings of the Regent and his
girls. He enlivened that retreat by agreeable relations with Mademoiselle de Corsambleu, who had a
taste for the stage, and who, four years later, made
her *début* in a production of Voltaire, *Artémire*.
The production and the *débutante* fell, the one upon
the other.

In the course of the year 1717, Voltaire, once more
in Paris, was accused, wrongly this time, of being
the author of a satire entitled *J'ai Vu* (I Have Seen),
which ended thus:

"I have seen, 'tis enough, the Jesuit adored."

The supposed author of the *J'ai Vu* was thrown
into the Bastille. There he composed the cantos of
his *Henriade*, and came out only in April, 1718.
The Marquess of Nocé, designing to save Voltaire
from exile, which was customary and of *right* after
an incarceration in the Bastille, sought to reconcile
him with the Regent, and conducted him to a reception at the Palais Royal. A storm burst out over-
head.

Voltaire, looking at the sky, cried out in the midst
of the courtiers:

"If a Regent governed up there, things could not
go on any worse!"

The Marquess of Nocé, when presenting Voltaire
to Philip of Orleans, said to him:

"My lord, this is the young Arouet whom you
have just taken out of the Bastille and whom you
are going to send there again;" and he related the
sally about the storm.

The Regent, who was as witty as licentious, philosopher in his own good hours, burst out with

laughter, and spoke of giving a pension to Voltaire,
who thus replied to him:

"I thank your Royal Highness for your bounty
in taking charge of my dinner-table, but I pray you
never more to provide my lodging."

However, Voltaire found it necessary to seek the
country air and to go to Châtenay, where his father
had engaged to have him watched over by one of
his relatives. After passing some time in that
forced retreat, he returned to the capital, and
brought out at the Theatre Français his tragedy of
Œdipe, which was applauded, and of which the two
following famous lines soon passed from mouth to
mouth:

"Our priests are not, in truth, what a vain people see ;
  Their craft is only born of our credulity."

Somewhat making light of his own production,
the author appeared upon the stage, carrying the
train of the high priest.

As soon as the work was printed, Voltaire sent a
copy of it to Jean Baptiste Rousseau, who answered
him from Brussels by a letter, of which we give the
conclusion :

"I would say a great many things concerning the
excellent work you have sent me. . . . But I
hope that we will meet in Brussels, and there have
the pleasure of discoursing upon many things which
would be too tedious to write."

In May, 1719, another harsh measure fell upon
Voltaire, to whom was attributed the Sophomoric
poem flung at the Regent, the *Philippics*. Voltaire
was once more banished from Paris. He led a wandering life, now at Sully, with the duke, now with

the *Maréchale* de Villars, with whom he fell in love, now in Touraine, at la Source, with Lord Bolingbroke, a man of learning and a Freethinker, banished from his country through the intrigues of the Jacobites, and who had married a French woman, Madame de Villette.

Thus went Voltaire, from castle to castle, conversing, devising, sowing wit upon his way, and ever working wherever he happened to be.

The following year his ban was raised, and he hurried back to Paris. But soon after another misfortune befell him. Voltaire, meeting at Versailles, at a ministerial dinner, the officer Beauregard, whose denunciations had caused his first *embastillement,* he exclaimed :

" I was well aware that spies were paid, but I did not know yet that their reward was to eat at the table of the minister."

Having resolved to take revenge for this cruel affront, Beauregard watched for the passage of Voltaire at the bridge of Sevres, took him unawares, riddled him with blows and wounded him in the face.

Voltaire asked for justice. The officer-spy had rejoined his regiment, and moreover he was protected by the minister.

From a letter sent by Voltaire to Cardinal Dubois, dated at Cambrai, July, 1722, we learn that he was the companion, the attendant of the Marchioness Julie de Rupelmonde during a pleasure tour in Belgium and Holland :

A beauty named Rupelmonde,
With whom the sly Cupid and I
Do roam of late *par tout le monde,*

> And who does o'er us lord it high,
> Commands that *instanter* I write. . . .

This marchioness, daughter of Marshal d'Aligre and widow of a rich lord of Flanders, to whom she had been married in 1705, was in full maturity, blonde, and sprightly. Voltaire had cured her from bigotry and from the zealots who love to console young widows, by converting her to philosophy. But to that she had added gallantry. To her it is that Voltaire had addressed the celebrated *Ode to Uranie*, which was at first the *Ode to Julia*, and some lines of which are subjoined:

> 'Tis then thy will, fair Uranie,
> That now, at thy behest, a new Lucretius born,
>   By my undaunted hand, for thee
> The bands of superstition may be torn;
>   That I expose to view the sad and dangerous sight
>   Of all the holy lies that fill the earth with blight,
> And that, imbued with my philosophy,
>   The horrors of the tomb thou mayest learn to scorn,
>   And all the foolish dread of the life yet unborn.

The fair widow and the witty philosopher, happy wandering couple, had a great struggle in tearing themselves away from the Cambrai *fêtes*, where a congress had assembled. But, however regretfully, they had to take their leave and cross the Belgian border. In Brussels, Voltaire repaired, *au débotté*, to the house of his friend, Jean Baptiste Rousseau, whom he thought he would find a Freethinker as in Paris, but *quantum mutatus ab illo!*

Rousseau was a skilful rhymer, of incontestable talent, but he did not possess the elevation of character and the nobility of soul of the true poet. He had returned to the bosom of the church, probably touched by Catholic grace during exile at Brussels, exile which he had brought to himself by his *Moside* (*Moïsade*), by his scurrillous pamphlets and licentious epigrams, leveled in Paris at everybody's head.

After the first expressions of friendship and the warm demonstrations of the two friends so much charmed once more to see each other, Voltaire proposed a promenade outside the city, and they mounted the carriage.

It is impossible for two poets to remain long together without speaking of their works and confiding their labors to each other. Voltaire read to Rousseau his " Ode to Julia." Hardly had he listened to the first strophe ere Jean Baptiste chose to become indignant with the "impious ideas" scattered in the piece, and threatened to leave the carriage in order to hear no more.

Voltaire derided the bigoted sentiments of which Rousseau made such a show before him, and exclaimed:

"Let us go to the play—but I regret that the author of the *Moïsade* did not inform the public that he had turned bigot."

It seems that during an interlude of the comedy, Rousseau read to Voltaire his "Ode to Posterity," yet unpublished, and consulted him concerning its value.

"Do you know, my master," ironically replied Voltaire, when he had ended, "that I do not believe that ode will ever reach its destination?"

Rousseau said not a word, and remained under the blow of that cutting epigram. He was wounded to the very core. The two poets parted in anger —sworn enemies. *Genus irritabile vatum!*

In the voluminous correspondence of Voltaire are found letters from Belgium dated in 1722, 1734, 1737, 1739, 1740, 1741, 1742, and 1744.

The correspondence of Voltaire (Edit. Beuchot) mentions only one letter addressed to Thierot, and dated September 11, 1722, in which he says to his friend that he will be again in Paris from Brussels within fifteen days, and that he will go to see Sully to have "the rascal snapped."

The rascal in question was the French officer, Beauregard.

Voltaire remained two weeks in Brussels, where, he writes, he was every day *en fête*, at which they did him the honors in an exquisite manner. After this he visited several cities of Belgium with Madame de Rupelmonde.' In Holland he met some publishers, and busied himself with the publication of the first cantos of his *Henriade*. He had been unable to find a publisher in France.

In the seventeenth and eighteenth centuries, Holland was one of the principal retreats of Free-thought. There it is that Locke and Shaftesbury, victims of the Jacobites and of the Catholic government of James II., came. Shaftesbury died there. It was at Amsterdam that Basnage, Bayle, Leclerc, l'Abbé Prevost, Rousseau, and many others, also sought a refuge. From the printing-presses of that free city of the United Provinces issued pamphlets, papers, and philosophical works, which afterwards spread over all Europe, making the Revolution in minds before its translation into facts.

His *voyage d'agrément* in company with his amiable marchioness being terminated, Voltaire turned toward Paris. He threw himself with feverish ardor into the noble studies, not without shooting his epigrams right and left and paying his court to the beautiful Duchesse de Villars, whom he still very much admired.

The Duchess was quite willing to discourse of tender things with the poet, but, like a great coquette, she held his passion at a distance in the Platonic spheres.

Voltaire, who had defined love as "the stuff of nature embroidered by the imagination," was on that chapter a little of the school of the Regency, more sensual than sentimental, if we except, however, his relations with Madame du Châtelet. From the too ethereal heights of the Duchesse de Villars he descended into Cythera with a very poor and very charming young girl, Mademoiselle Suzanne Livry. It was a veritable romance of youth. Suzanne became for him a new Pimpette. She wished to consecrate herself to the theatre. Voltaire told her that comedy was synonymous with love and passion, and asked her if she had loved. Upon her answering in the negative, the poet taught her the play and comedy of love.

Some months elapsed. Suzanne took a part in the comedy of Voltaire. Then she committed several infidelities against the author, and left with a company of comedians for London. But the enterprise failed. Suzanne fell into poverty—and into the arms of the rich and original Marquess of Gouvernet, who met her in an obscure London tavern and wedded her. Voltaire has made that incident the subject of his *Ecossaise*.

Near the end of his life Voltaire had the whim of going to visit, in her hotel at Paris, the Marchioness of Gouvernet. But she did not receive him. He was stopped at the door by a large and solemn lackey. Voltaire sent her the charming and satirical poem of the *Vous* and the *Tu*, contrasting the measured coldness of the Marchioness with the abandon and carelessness of the *ex-comédienne* of the ruby lips:

"Ah, Phyllis! where is now the time
    When in a cab we rode about;
No footmen, no adornments thine,
    Beyond thine own, all charms without;
With a bad supper, blithe and free,
    Which thou for me ambrosian made;
Thou gavest thyself all to me,
    A happy dupe, ah, fickle maid!
With all my life enwrapped in thee?

. . . .

" For treasures all, as well as rank,
    The Fates alone thou hadst to thank,
For beauty common to thy age,
A tender heart, not very sage,
A marble breast and beauteous eyes—
With all these charms, a precious prize;
    Alas! who roguish would not be ?
Thou wert, ah, graceful, wicked nymph!
    Yet (may Cupid forgive it me,)
I loved thee but the more, thou imp."

For her only answer,' the Marchioness sent the poet's portrait painted in his youth.

" Oh, my friends !" exclaimed Voltaire, reporting his visit; "I have just passed from one shore of the Cocytus to the other."

Voltaire's relations with Adrienne Lecouvereur lasted a little longer than the ones he had carried on with the fickle Suzanne Livry. It was in the presence of that famous comedienne, at her house or in her box at the opera, that he had an altercation with a pretentious sot called the Chevalier de Rohan-Chabot. Having acted impertinently toward the poet, he was nailed to the wall by one of those cutting replies which were habitual with Voltaire.

"Who might be that young man who speaks in such a high key?" the Chevalier is reported to have asked.

"He is," replied Voltaire, "a man who is establishing his name while you are finishing yours."

Two days after, Voltaire, dining with the Duke of Sully, was called outside, drawn into an ambush, and bastinadoed by the lackeys of the Chevalier de Rohan, who was present at the execution of his orders, and ended by saying to his rabble:

"It is enough!"

Voltaire, mad with rage, vainly demanded reparation for that shameful outrage from the miserable knight, from God and devil. "Justice has been done!" was the reply everywhere.

Knowing that Voltaire was practicing fencing, and wished to force him to accept a duel, the Chevalier de Rohan induced the minister to have his mortal enemy shut up in the Bastille. That second incarceration lasted a year. Voltaire came out of prison in August, 1726, to be embarked at Calais, by order of the lieutenant of police, and to sail for England.

It was during that year, 1726, that he is supposed to have renounced the name of Arouet and to have taken, from some estate, the one he has rendered illustrious.

II.

Voltaire, banished from France, chose for his residence London, where existed neither Bastille nor
bastinadoes for philosophers, nor Jesuits to prevent
their speech, and where, to use his own expression,
" reason knew no restraint."

England was then full of Freethinkers and Whigs.

An ancestor, a father of free thought, Shaftesbury, was dead, as well as the celebrated philosopher
Locke, the author of the "Essay on the Understanding," the apostle of political and religious liberty.
But Toland, Collins, Wollaston, and Tindal were yet
living when Voltaire landed in London. Bolingbroke, pardoned, had returned from France. Wollaston had just published his "Discourse Against the
Miracles of Jesus Christ," the journalist, Richard
Steele, colleague of Addison in the *Spectator*, his
ringing pamphlets, and Bolingbroke, his learned criticisms on Christianity.

Politics, philosophy, science, letters, all flourished,
all were fruitful, ripened by the sun of liberty, by
the rays of that great Revolution of 1688, which
had put an end to absolute power and given wing to
English genius. Thus thinkers, writers, publicists
now saw all roads opened before them. Far from
being persecuted, gagged, and castigated, as in
France, they could aspire to the highest charges.

The electrifying effect produced by emancipated
England upon our fugitive from the Bastille, upon

the man just out of the French trap, will be easily imagined. What dazzling brightness, what feast of thought for Voltaire entering the modern Athens! From the darkness he was emerging into the light, from the midst of courtiers and slaves he found himself suddenly transported into a land of free men, organizing their activities in all independence.

The English, with their self-government under George I., their freedom of meetings, of association, of the press, of political and religious propaganda, presented a perfect contrast to the French bent under the royal *bonplaisir* and the Jesuitic arbitrary will. The frank, bold, impetuous character of the Englishman captivated Voltaire.

He drank with avidity from the British tankard the nectar which strengthened his powerful faculties and gave a solid basis to his mind. He devoured everything, books, pamphlets, journals, speeches, sermons. He attended meetings, gatherings, circles. His laborious and studious life was at that period, he has said, the life of a Rosicrucian, "ever hidden, ever on the march."

Carlyle informs us, in his "History of Frederick the Great," that upon his arrival in London, Voltaire lived for some time in an old house, inhabited to this day, in Maiden Lane, Covent Garden. He was very cordially received at Wandsworth, in the cottage of an opulent merchant of London, a friend of letters and well read himself, Mr. Fawkener.

The houses of the great were not slow to open themselves for the French exile. He was received with the utmost cordiality at Pall-Mall, in the sumptuous mansion of Bolingbroke, and in his residence at Dawley.

Voltaire remained three weeks with Lord Peters-borough. He also very assiduously frequented the house of Pope, the illustrious author of the "Essay on Man," and whom he estimated "the most elegant, correct, and harmonious poet of England."

At the homes of Lord Bolingbroke, Lord Peters-borough, and Pope, Voltaire found himself in rela-tions with nearly all the British celebrities—with Clarke, Gay, Congreve, Thomson, Young, Swift, whom he called the English Rabelais. In that circle of brilliant minds philosophical discussions some-times became very lively. According to his wont, Voltaire put a slight curb upon the expression of his thoughts. At one of Pope's great dinners, if we must believe an English chronicler, he treated Chris-tianity in such a cavalier way that Pope's mother, a good Catholic, rose from the table and withdrew. Admitting the authenticity of this incident, it did not interrupt his good relations with Pope.

Lastly, Voltaire dwelt in Beletery Square with a certain Cavalier. It is not probable, however, that it was the hero of the Cévennes, who, in Holland, had been his rival in his love affair with Pimpette.

It would appear that Lady Laura Harley had much inclination and admiration for Voltaire. But this cosmopolitan English woman had for appendix a very jealous husband—a true Othello, who very quickly put an end to the romance.

Voltaire placed himself in relations with all the personages of mark and originality; political and literary men, poets and philosophers. He did not even omit to see and frequent the Quakers.

Among other visits of Voltaire, his commentators speak, in their memoirs, of his interviews with the famous comic author, Congreve, the German Fabrice, Lady Sundon, and the Princess Caroline. He charmed every one, and gained his city right by the vivacity and the brightness of his wit, his tact, his *ton* of man of the world, and also, it must be said, by amiable flatteries, which he dropped upon his way, as formerly Buckingham threw pearls at the feet of admiring belles.

Voltaire knew, in London, the celebrated Duchess of Marlborough, then occupied with the editing of her "Memoirs." But he failed to see the greatest scientific genius of the eighteenth century—the *legislator of the heavens*, he who had subdued the world to the great law of universal attraction—Isaac Newton, already sick at the time of his arrival. On the 25th of March, 1727, he assisted at his sumptuous obsequies with all England, pondering, perhaps, that in France Moliere had been denied a sepulture.

Upon landing, the first care of the exile was to perfect himself in the study of the English tongue; and well it was, for had he been ignorant of it, the London population, who hated the French, would have treated him badly.

One day he was followed by a group of furious workingmen, who aimed at nothing less than stoning the *Frenchman*. Voltaire, in close quarters, did not lack presence of mind. He mounted a stone, and harangued his pursuers: "Worthy Englishmen," said he, "is it not misfortune enough not to have been born among you?" . . .

At the end of his allocution, the populace, flattered, passed from wrath to enthusiasm. But Voltaire, knowing the versatility of the mob, prudently escaped.

Some time after, he was the victim of a much more serious accident. /Entering the office of the Jew d'Acosta to cash a cheque of 20,000 francs drawn upon him, and which he wrongly had neglected to present, the son of Abraham informed him that he had declared bankruptcy the day preceding. / Happily, King George hearing of this misadventure of Voltaire, spontaneously sent him 100 guineas, which put him out of difficulty. At the same time, his poem, "La Henriade," was made ready for publication by subscription. Heading the list were the names of the royal family and all the court. Bolingbroke having declined the honor of the dedication, the "Henriade" was dedicated to the queen. It had such a success that three editions were taken up at once. The author realized important sums, which, later in France, he placed in fruitful commercial operations. Among other services, the English Positivists developed in him the genius of business. But it is rather curious that the publication of an epic poem was the beginning of Voltaire's fortune.

During his three years' sojourn in London Voltaire profoundly studied the institutions, the customs, and the manners of England. He became initiated into the philosophy of Locke, which brought all human knowledge back to the sole source of subjective and objective experience. He studied the works and the system of Newton, who had scattered the famous and fantastic world-mists of Descartes. He was strongly impressed by reading Shakspere in the original. It is true that he did not appreciate the true value of his genius, and that he qualified as barbarous the fiery *élans* of the English dramatist, which disturbed the classic *convenu* of the eighteenth century. It was Voltaire, nevertheless, who revealed Shakspere to Europe, which was ignórant of him, and the meditation of his works must certainly have benefited the author of "Brutus," "Zaire," and "Mahomet."

M. Villemain, in his "Tableau de la Littérature au XVIIIe Siecle," estimates as follows English influence upon Voltaire and the French thinkers:

"Bolingbroke was pardoned in 1726, and returned to London. Voltaire, emerging from the Bastille, joined him there. This was the time when the young president of Montesquieu made the same voyage, in the company of Lord Chesterfield. England, from 1723 to 1730, was thus the school of the two first master-minds of that century. Later, Buffon began his great researches of nature through the study and translation of English discoveries. The most active mind after Voltaire, Diderot, borrowed of England his first studies and his first "Essai d'Encyclopédie." Jean Jacques Rousseau drew from the works of Locke a great part of his ideas upon politics and education. Condillac owes to them all his philosophy."

Formed, fashioned, kneaded, as it were, by English science, literature, philosophy, and legislation, Voltaire returned to France very different from what he was when he had left it. The three years of his exile in that great and free country had opened for him new and large horizons, had given him an intellectual vigor, a tempered mind, a moral force, which became apparent when he was at last permitted to return to his fatherland.

The French minister, favorably considering a demand of Voltaire, based upon the imperious necessity of regulating matters of interest, had signed, on the 29th of July, 1727, the following authorization :

"Permission to the *sieur* de Voltaire to come to Paris to attend to his affairs during three months, to begin with the day of his arrival; and said time being elapsed, it is to him enjoined by his majesty to return to the place of his exile, under penalty of disobedience. (Dated at Versailles, and signed)
"PHILYPEAUX."

As he himself tells us, without giving his motives, Voltaire did not utilize that permit of sojourn in Paris, since he remained in London until the spring of 1729, at which time the new minister, De Maurepas, no longer opposed his return.

III.

New trials awaited Voltaire in France. The 11th
of September, 1730, he put upon the stage his " Brutus," written in London and dedicated to Lord Bolingbroke. The piece had some success, although it
was found too republican.

Voltaire did not cease to criticise the abuses and
the moral and material servitudes of his country, by
exalting English liberties. His enthusiasm for Great
Britain eloquently betrayed itself in his "Ode à
Lecouvreur " (October, 1731), which avenged the
memory of the famous comedienne clandestinely interred at La Grenouillère, after a refusal of sepulture
from the clergy. We publish *in extenso* that admirable ode, in which Voltaire praises England as
warmly as the great tragic actress of the eighteenth
century.

Here let us note a remarkable particular : This
piece was set to music by the Prince Royal of Prussia, Frederick, who was a *maestro* of the first order,
and played the flute to a charm.

ODE TO ADRIENNE LECOUVREUR.

What do I see? Great God! Those lips soft as the lyre,
O God! these heavenly eyes, the source of living fire,
Of death are made to know the livid horrors now.
O muses, graces, loves of whom she was the type,
My gods and hers, O help! for death can she be ripe?
But what is this? 'Tis done! Alas! thou art laid low—
Yes, dead! and all have learnt thou art beyond relief.
All hearts with mine are moved, are filled with mortal grief.

I hear on every side the arts thy fate deplore
And cry, with tearful eyes, "Melpomene is no more!"
        What will you say, O future race,
When you the insult know, which naught can e'er efface,
Now offered by vile men to these arts sad distressed?
        They have refused a resting-place
To one for whom of old her altars Greece had dressed.
Before she left the world they all for her would sigh;
Their bondage I beheld, on her I saw them fawn.
Did then her crime begin when cruel death came nigh?
Is it for charming you she's punished, now she's gone?
No more for us shall be this an unholy glade,
For therein lies thy form, and this, thy sad, last home,
E'er honored by our strains, and hallowed by thy shade,
        A holy temple will become.
Here is my St. Denys; 'tis here that I adore
Thy talent and thy wit, thy charms, thy winning grace.
I loved them when thou wert, I shall honor them more
        In spite of death's most foul embrace—
        In spite of error, or ingrates
Who could alone thy wrong to share with thee deplore.
Oh! must I ever see my nation, weak and vain,
Uncertain in its vows, disgrace what we admire;
Our deeds upon our laws e'er stand as a satire;
And fickle sons of France beneath the dark empire
        Of superstition lain?
        Is it upon the English strand
        Alone that thought can dare be free?
O Athens' rival, thou, O London, happy land!
Just as thy tyrants fled, thou hast compelled to flee
The shameful herd that warr'd against free thought and
        thee.
'Tis there men know all things to say and to reward;
No art is there despised; all skill commands regard;
The hero of Tallard, of victory favored son,
And Dryden the sublime, and Addison the wise,
Ophils with charms replete, the immortal Newton,
        To Memory's shrine together rise.
In England, Lecouvreur would have been laid to rest
Among her heroes, kings, her greatest and her best.

For talent there insures a place 'neath fame's high dome,
    And freedom, with resources hived,
    Has, after centuries, on Albion's shore revived
    The soul of Greece and Rome.
What! shall we never more upon our fields, grown tame,
Apollo's laurel leaf upspringing hope to see?
Immortal gods! why has my country ceased to be
    The home of worth and fame?

The sharp critique made by the poet upon clerical intolerance, on the score of their refusal of inhumation for Lecouvreur, answered perfectly to the public feeling. But it was not without danger when all-powerful priests governed the State and the woman Louis XV.

It is at this period that happened the scandalous case of the Jesuit Girard. The confessor of a young and handsome Tolosian, Catherine Cadière, the reverend father had seduced her by means of a gross mysticism—by persuading her that sister-souls could unite and mingle their bodies; that God had commanded him to blow in her mouth and administer the discipline upon her naked body. The pretty penitent was made to enter a convent, where the relations were continued. La Cadière was soon in an interesting way, gave birth to a precocious monk, and *Father* Girard was forced to render account of his mystic operations before the parliament.

After his ode to Lecouvreur, Voltaire had prudently sought refuge for a few months in Normandy.

In the month of October, 1732, the first representation of Zaïre—that enchanting drama, has said a critic—proved a sparkling triumph, and consecrated his fame as a dramatic author. But the laurels of Voltaire were ever interwoven with thorns. The publication of his letter to Uranie, written ten years earlier, raised the indignation of the godly party. The archbishop of Paris, M. de Vintemille, addressed a complaint to the lieutenant of police upon the scandal of the Voltairian epistle. Chancellor d'Aguesseau consulted on this subject his secretary, Langlois, who answered him:

"My lord, Voltaire should be shut up in a place where he could never have either pen, ink, or paper. By the turn of his mind that man can ruin a State."

Voltaire called at the ministerial bar, having found an escape-flue. He repudiated the paternity of the ode, which he attributed to the late Abbé de Chaulieu. Without taking him at his word, they rested content with the excuse.

But, some time later, more ado. Not a production of Voltaire's could appear without creating a tempest. His "Temple du Goût," a witty and amusing poem, half verse, half prose, alienated against him all the lettered and courtier tribe. It was a vigorous satire upon false taste and the absurd infatuations of the period, filled with allusions, waggery, and keen darts launched at his enemies, upon the ephemeral idols of the public, and a few popular authors, who, rendered furious, answered him by insulting letters, epigrams, pamphlets, and parodies.

The author of the "Temple du Goût" enjoyed all this frenzy, attesting that he had struck at the very defect in the cuirass, and meanwhile was completing his "Lettres sur les Anglais," commenced in London—a perfect revelation of political, philosophical, scientific, and literary England, hitherto unknown in France. He extolled Newton's system, Locke's philosophy, the liberties, the religious tolerance, of

Outre Manche. With the privileges, the despotism, and the abuses of the French system he contrasted the free institutions and customs of England. He thrashed the French priests upon the backs of the Anglican clergy by writing:

"The Anglican clergy has retained many Catholic ceremonies, and especially that of collecting the tithes with the most attentive scrupulousness. The Anglicans have also the pious desire of being masters; for what vicar does not wish to be pope?"

In his "Frederick the Great," Carlyle declares very correct Voltaire's appreciation of the English and of England in the eighteenth century.

Several manuscript copies of Voltaire's work had circulated with impunity. But the editor, *Jore fils*, having published the "Lettres sur les Anglais," under the name of "Lettres Philosophiques," he was thrown into the Bastille. Referred to parliament, the book was condemned as "scandalous, contrary to religion, to good morals, to the respect due to the powers," and publicly burned by the hand of the executioner. A writ of arrest was issued against its author, but he was not found at his lodgings. At that moment he was in Monjeu, assisting at the celebration of the marriage of the Duke of Richelieu with Mademoiselle de Guise. A *lettre de cachet* commanded the author of the "Lettres Philosophiques" to constitute himself prisoner in the Château d'Auxonne, near Dijon.

"I have a mortal aversion against the jail," wrote Voltaire. "I am sick; confined air would have killed me. They would perhaps have stuck me in a cell. . . . What makes me believe the orders were severe is that the Marshalsea was astir."

Voltaire avoided that extremity by leaving Paris
and hiding in an unknown place. But he suddenly
emerged from his retreat to join the army, when he
learned that the Duke of Richelieu had been wounded in a duel with the Prince of Liscin, who had been
stretched on the ground. Arrived at the camp of
Philipsbourg, he found Richelieu, slightly wounded,
who feasted him, in company with the Prince of
Conti and of the Counts of Charolois and of Cler-
mont. They passed from the festal board to the
battle-field. Voltaire braved musket-balls and can-
non-shot. But, being taken for a spy, he came near
being executed. Recognizing the dangers of his
presence at the camp, he took refuge in the castle of
Cirey, in Champagne, in the retreat offered him by
the Marchioness Emilie du Châtelet. Voltaire, who
called her a very amiable and calumniated woman,
had gained her friendship by dedicating to her his
" Epître Contre la Calomnie."

At that time Mme. du Châtelet was in Paris, seeking to put to work influences in favor of Voltaire
and to calm the tempest. She wrote :

" I am entirely convinced that the minister has a
well-formed design to ruin him. They speak of banishment. For me, I know that in his place I should
have been in London or at Hague long ago."

Whether he did not believe himself safe, or was
weary of living alone in that desert of Cirey, surrounded by mountains and uncultivated land, according to the portraiture of Madame Denis, Voltaire
sought refuge in Belgium. He remained there one
month. From Brussels he wrote two letters to the
Count of Argental, dated in the month of November,
1734, in which he shows his impatience to learn the

issue of the interview which Madame de Richelieu was to have concerning him with the lord-keeper of the great seal, and also of the attempt in the same direction made by Madame du Châtelet. "For my part," he ends with, "I admit to you that I shall have to possess great philosophic resignation in order to forget the unworthy manner in which I have been treated by my country."

Feeling more secure, he returns to Cirey, where he finds the châtelaine Emilie and several distinguished visitors. Voltaire soon becomes the god of that circle. He throws down wit and mirth by handfuls. In the evenings he makes the guests of Cirey swell with laughter by showing them the magic lantern, by causing these Chinese profiles to play all the intrigues of the times, by running dialogues in the most comic Savoyard accent. Dramas were also represented at Cirey. Amateur comedy was, as every one knows, one of the passions of the eighteenth century. Madame du Châtelet appeared on the stage, and played her part royally well; which did not prevent her from studying the exact sciences, to Newtonize, whilst Voltaire elaborated his works.

IV.

Ever reappearing on the Parisian arena, and ceaselessly taking up again his warp of Penelope,
Voltaire put on the stage, in 1736, "Alzire" and
"l'Enfant Prodigies." Emboldened, Voltaire solicit-
ed a second time a chair at the Academy; but his
enemies leagued against him, and caused him once
more to fail. He felt very sensitive over this check.

At the end of the year 1736, two reasons forced
Voltaire to disappear temporarily from France—a
moral reason and a political reason. The swelling
and pullulating pack of the Jesuits and bigots accused him of sacrilege and barked at his heels for
having said in his publication of the *Mondain* that
Adam had finger-nails of the length of those of an
ape, and having made our mother Eve the object of
keen pleasantries. On the other hand, the relatives
of Madame du Châtelet had found scandalous his
presence at the castle of Cirey and his intimacy with
the châtelaine, in the absence of her husband, the
Marquess of Châtelet, who was with the army.

For these reasons, and especially because he felt
weary of hiding and being tracked about, tired of
living with the invariable prospective of the Bastille
and of a writ, Voltaire was pushed to seek a tempo-
rary security in Belgium and Holland. The Prince
Royal of Prussia had, indeed, offered him a refuge,
but Madame du Châtelet dissuaded him from accept-
ing it. She put under key his manuscript of the

"Pucelle," which Voltaire intended to take with him to have it printed in Holland.

"It is necessary at every turn to save him from himself," she wrote, "and I use more diplomacy to guide him than all the Vatican employs to keep the Christian world in bonds."

Madame du Châtelet was really too prudent concerning Voltaire, and, with her precautions, she would have extinguished his genius, had it been extinguishable.

The very day of his passage to Brussels, the 16th of January, 1737, one of his pieces, "Alzire," was being played.

"His laurels follow him everywhere," observed the Marchioness of Châtelet to the Count d'Argental. "But what does so much glory profit him? Obscure happiness would be much preferable. *O vana hominum mentes! O pectora cœca!*"

Madame du Châtelet understands here, by "obscure happiness," the happy days which Voltaire spent with her at the Château de Cirey; which he charmed with his witty conversation, as Madame de Graffigny said, adding that being deprived of Voltaire's small-talk was a real punishment.

Voltaire, arrived in Brussels, remained there but a short while. M. Desnoireterres, the learned author of "Voltaire and French Society in the Eighteenth Century," attributes his short residence to the unpleasantness which, it is said, he experienced at meeting there his declared enemy, the poet Jean Baptiste Rousseau. Their quarrel had, indeed, become very much envenomed since the year 1722, and had taken the character of a mortal fray.

Rousseau had narrated according to his point of

view their altercations of 1722. He pretended that
it was the impiety of Voltaire, his attacks upon
Christianity, which had revolted him. But in reality
it was his slaying epigram upon the "Ode à la Pos-
terité." He reproached him with being a follower
of the Marchioness de Rupelmonde, and with not
having had with her Platonic relations alone.
He added that he had introduced Voltaire into
several great families of Brussels, and that his
manners there had been improper. In the church
of the Sablons, he would have it appear, Voltaire
had troubled the service and listened very undevout-
ly to the mass. He charged Voltaire, furthermore,
with having blattered against him at Marimont, and
with having at Mons so much incensed the *table
d'hôte* by his words that he came near being thrown
out of the window.

Rousseau, besides, had attributed to Voltaire the
odious project of going to preach Atheism in the
Netherlands, bringing forward to support his calumnies the learned Sr. Gravesand and the Duke of
Aremberg; both of whom opposed him with an express denial.

Lastly, a violent pamphlet from Rousseau had
appeared in a Paris magazine.

Voltaire, however, was not at all behind his charitable *confrère*. He had riddled him with epigrams,
notably in his "Temple du Goût." To his pamphlet
he had replied by his deoppilating "Crepinade." To
understand the piquant allusion in this title, it must
be known that Rousseau was the son of a shoemaker
of Paris, and that, the honest man having come to
the *foyer* to congratulate him after his first representation of the "Flatteur" at the Theater Fran-

çais, Rousseau, swollen with pride, had refused to recognize him. He did not want to be known as the son of an artisan.

Here is the biased appreciation of the difference between Voltaire and Rousseau, made by a Catholic writer, M. Capefigue:

"Rousseau, the poet so long exiled for his impieties and sarcasms, was now growing old. What a change had been operated in him! Proscribed on account of an abominable book attributed to him, the 'Moïsade,' Rousseau had taken refuge in Belgium, and he was expiating in Brussels, by sacred odes and some sublime strophies, the wanderings of his youth. Voltaire had visited him a moment in Belgium; they had been again drawn together by a mutual correspondence, soon suddenly interrupted. They agreed no longer. Voltaire was commencing his career of impiety, Rousseau was ending his."

In the eyes of M. Capefigue, as in the minds of all his co-religionists, it is impiety to defend liberty of thought.

Voltaire had gone from Brussels to Anvers, in Holland, where he had embarked upon the canals. He took the name of Révol, and had his correspondence addressed to the care of MM. Ferney and d'Arty, merchants of Amsterdam. But he lived with Ledet, who printed an edition of his works, comprising the "Eléments de la Philosophie de Newton," uncompleted. Voltaire went to Leyden, where he chose his domicile with a banker named Rollen. In Berlin he saw the celebrated physician Boerhaave.

During this time, Madame du Châtelet imparts her mortal inquietudes to the Count of Argental, whom

Voltaire called his good angel, and who was, indeed,
all his life the type of the devoted and disinterested
friend.   In her letters dated from Cirey she entreats
him to use all his influence upon his friend to dissuade him from incorporating the "Mondain" in the
edition of his works, and to divert him from visiting
Prussia.

"His sojourn in Prussia would harm him," says
she. "The climate is horribly cold. The Prince
Royal is not king.   When he shall be king, we shall
go to see him *together*.   But until he is, there is no
security there.   His father knows no other merit
than that of being ten feet high; . . . he is sus-
picious and cruel; he hates and persecutes his son;
he keeps him under a yoke of iron."

The Châtelaine de Cirey has such a fear of Voltaire going to Prussia that she does not leave him
time to complete the "Eléments de la Philosophie
de Newton" at Amsterdam. She sends him letter
after letter to recall him to Cirey, to the effect that
Voltaire believes himself in duty bound to defer to
her wishes. This recall to the gardens of Armida
was not of long duration.

V.

Marc-Antoine du Châtelet, Marquess of Trichâ-
teau, had just died, bequeathing to his cousin his
properties situated in Flanders.   This succession
gave rise to serious litigation between the houses
of Châtelet and of Hoensbroeck. In order to sustain
a suit and to defend her endangered interests, the
Marchioness du Châtelet unhesitatingly left Cirey,

with her inseparable Voltaire, who was not sorry to breathe more freely abroad than in France, where he was ever disturbed, threatened, and forced to concealment.

Leaving Cirey on the 8th of May, 1739, the two travelers arrived at Brussels on the 28th, after having stopped four or five days at Valenciennes. Voltaire and the Marchioness scarcely touched land at Brussels. They went at once, passing by Louvain, to Bevinghen, whence Madame du Châtelet wrote to the Count d'Argental:

"Here we are in Flanders, my dear friend. I was visited and feasted in Brussels when I merely passed. Rousseau is no more spoken of there than if he were dead. All were eager to feast M. de Voltaire. I am actually within ten leagues of Brussels, on an estate of M. du Châtelet."

Then Voltaire sought the most quiet quarter in Brussels, and installed himself, with Madame du Châtelet, in the Rue de la Grosse Tour (Great Tower Street).*

She was a precious companion for a philosopher,

---

* To-day the Rue du Grand Cerf (Great Deer street). A tavern exists yet to-day, bearing the sign: "A la Grosse Tour." In 1742 and 1743 Voltaire lived in Brussels, Place de Louvain, as is attested by the letter he wrote, in a pleasant Oriental style, to the Abbe Aumillon, in October, 1742, and ending thus:

"Written in my pigmy closet, Place de Louvain, afflicted with an enormous colic, the 8th of the moon of the 9th month, the year of the hegira 1122."

On the other hand, Madame du Châtelet was writing from Lille to the Count d'Argental, the 10th of October, 1743:

"I am going to Brussels as soon as a slight fever I have is over. Write me at Brussels, Place de Louvain."

this young and admirable woman, impassioned with science, possessing upon the ends of her fingers all the Greek and Latin authors, and translating into French the works of Newton. She had Koenig, her professor of mathematics, to follow her to Brussels.

Notwithstanding his resolution to isolate himself in order to be fully consecrated to his cherished studies and noble labors, Voltaire did not long remain secluded in Brussels. Rousseau had, the very first thing, let out his presence in the capital of Brabant. He went clamoring everywhere against the illustrious writer, repeating that he preached Atheism.

Jealous of Voltaire's fame, Rousseau had vainly sought to divert the Duke d'Aremburg from the society of the author of "Zaïre," whom he cavalierly styled a *rimeur de deus jours*, or "a forty-eight hour rhymer." Voltaire, to whom repartee was an easy thing, retorted by comparing Rousseau's poetry to the croaking of frogs.

All that Rousseau gained by his calumnies and hostilities against Voltaire was the loss of the pension generously given him by the Duke d'Aremberg, and expulsion from his house.

To conclude with Rousseau, let us say that, struck with apoplexy on his return from Hague in the month of October, 1740, he died in Brussels on the 17th of March, 1741, at the respectable age of seventy-one, and that his piety brought him the honor of being interred in the church of the Bare-footed Carmelites.

Piron, who had the mania of epitaphs to such a degree that he composed his own—

" Here lies Pirou, who naught could be,
  Not even Academician be "—

also wrote Rousseau's epitaph. It has remained
famous. We subjoin it:

" Here lies the illustrious, unfortunate Rousseau;
  In Paris he was born, and in Brabant laid low.
  His life is in this epitaph
  Summed up: It was too long by half.
  For thirty years of envy worthy,
  For thirty more he was to pity."

The judgment of Pirou may be accepted as impar-
tial, for the author of the " Metromanie " was the
intimate friend of Jean Baptiste Rousseau, from
whom he did not separate during his sojourn in
Brussels in 1738 and 1740. In these two years Pirou
did not see Voltaire. He was secretly jealous of
him, and, blinded by his immense vanity, pretended
to be his superior. " Voltaire works in marquetry,"
said he, " and I cast in bronze."

But let us retrace our steps and return to the year
1739.

Jean Baptiste Rousseau had vainly used all his
venom-teeth against the finely-tempered file of Voltaire, whom the most distinguished personages of
Brussels knew well how to appreciate, as well as to
find his peaceful retreat in the Rue de la Grosse
Tour; among others, the Prince of Chimai, the
Duke of Aremberg, who became his friends, and the
grandson of the illustrious pensionary De Witt, who
put at his disposition his library—the richest in
Europe. Desirous of requiting these courteous visits, Voltaire gave a feast, to which he invited the
representatives of several great Brussels families.
They responded with eagerness to his appeal.

"This is the country of uniformity," writes Voltaire to M. Berger, at the date of the 28th of June, 1739. "Brussels has so little activity that the greatest news of the day is a very small feast which I give to Madame du Châtelet, to Madame the Princess of Chimai, and to M. le Duc d'Aremberg. Rousseau, I believe, will have no share in it. It is assuredly the first feast given by a poet at his own expense, and where there was no poetry. I had promised a very gallant device for the fireworks, but I have had made some great and very luminous letters that say: 'I am for the *jeu va tout!*' That will not cure our ladies, who love the gleek a little too well. Yet I did it only to cure them."

This letter, by which we learn that the ladies of Brussels of the last century loved and played with frenzy the *brelan*, the *jeu va tout*, is followed, two days later, by another missive to Thiérot, in which Voltaire relates the tragic accident which had come to sadden the feast:

"I write you from a house from which Rousseau has been driven forever—a just punishment of his calumnies. I would say a good many things to you, but I am really sick from a shock which made me nearly faint when I saw fall at my feet, from the third story, two carpenters whom I had at work. Imagine what it is to see two poor artisans fall in this way and to be covered with their blood. I see that it is not for me to give entertainments. That sad spectacle corrupted all pleasure of the most agreeable journey in the world."

To chase away the impression of the terrible accident which had disturbed the sensibility of Voltaire, the Duke d'Aremberg had taken him, with Emilie, to his residence, d'Enghien.

If we believe Voltaire, the signification of the word *Utopia* was absolutely unknown in Brussels during the last century. Ignorant of the word, they of course were ignorant of the thing. And truly, they have never been very Utopian in Belgium. Here follows what Voltaire wrote to Helvetius on this subject:

"I admit to you with shame that I have never read the 'Utopia' of Thomas More. However, I took it in my head some days ago to give a merry-making in Brussels, under the name of the Envoy of Utopia. The feast was in honor of Madame du Châtelet, as a matter of course. But would you believe that nobody could be found in the town who knew the meaning of Utopia. It is not the home of belles-lettres."

One of the first thoughts of Voltaire in Belgium had been for Frederick, the Prince Royal of Prussia, to whom he had written a short letter as early as the 30th of May, from Louvain, during his excursion to Beringhen. In the first part of June, 1739, he addressed him a long missive, from which we extract what follows:

"Madame du Châtelet will do nothing here but plead. She will find very few persons to whom she can speak of philosophy. The arts do not dwell in Brussels any more than pleasures. A retired and quiet life is here the lot of nearly all individuals. But this quiet life simulates *ennui* so nearly that one can very easily mistake it."

The same critical idea of Brussels and Belgium is reproduced in several letters of Voltaire. Among

others is an epistle addressed, at a later period, to
M. de Farmont, and of which we give a stanza :

> " For the sorry town whence I write thee,
>   Of ignorance 'tis the home,
>   And, besides, of dullness and *ennui;*
>   Stupidity here reigns alone.
>
> 'Tis a land of true servility,
>   With no wit, and saintly to the core;
>   But then Emilie is here with me,
>   And she is alone worth France and more."

In a letter to Madame de Champbonin is found
this passage :

"There are, as you know, many princes in Brussels, and few men. One hears at every moment,
'Your Highness,' 'Your Excellency.'"

VI.

With his rapid glance and his habitual vivacity, Voltaire contents himself with exposing the penury of arts and letters in the Belgium of the eighteenth century; but to have been absolutely just he should have indicated the causes which had made of that intelligent and expressive race a nation of mutes, and had temporarily weaned them from their native qualities. Political and religious despotism is the grave-digger of nations, and liberty is their emancipator, their creator, as was so well proven at that period by the prosperity of the United Provinces, toward which all that Flanders had of vivaciousness and intelligence had been directing its course for a century.

Voltaire, then, should have recalled and placed by the side of his strictures upon the moral and intellectual state of Belgium in his time the vital explosion, the magnificent efflorescence, of the Flemish communes of the thirteenth and fourteenth centuries. Led by Artevelde, who at that period conceived the idea of the federal communes of Europe, they heroically resisted the oppression of the counts of Flanders, backed by the French monarchy, and succumbed only under the weight of overwhelming numbers, at Roesbeck, in 1382. Voltaire should have recalled the dark silhouettes of Philip II. and the Duke of Alva, swaying the ax over the head of all intelligence, over the heads which arose above

the level of servitude—principally over the members
of the Chambers of Rhetoric, which were a nursery
of poets and authors.

The Prince Royal of Prussia joined the chorus
with Voltaire against Brussels.   It is true he did not
spare Germany any more.

"Brussels, and nearly all Germany," he wrote to
Voltaire on the 17th of July, 1739, "still feel the
effects of their ancient barbarism.   They honor the
arts very little, and therefore cultivate them but
little.   The nobility bear arms, or, after superficial
studies, enter the bar, which they look upon as a
pleasant thing.   The well-to-do gentry live in the
country or in the woods, which makes them as wild
as the animals they pursue. . . . You must be
much more sensitive than any one else to the difference in the life of Paris and Brussels—you who
breathe only in the centers of art, who have brought
together in Cirey all that is most voluptuous, most
piquant in intellectual pleasures."

A letter of Voltaire to the Marquess of Argens,
dated July 18, 1739, relates the case of the Jesuit
Janssens, which at that time was making a great
noise :

"My compliments, dear friend, to the reverend
father Janssens, Jesuit, of Brussels, who persuaded
the poor dame Viana that her husband had died a
heretic, that consequently she could not in good
conscience keep any money in her possession, and
that she should place it all in the hands of her confessor.   The good lady Viana, full of compunction,
trusted all her money to him.   The coachman who
helped the reverend father to carry the sack gives
legal evidence against the reverend father.   The

good man says he does not know what it means, and prays God for them. The people, however, want to stone the saint. The case is going to be tried. He must be hung or canonized, and haply he will be the one and the other. Adieu, and let us be neither the one nor the other."

Voltaire and the Marchioness had left the shades of Enghien to return to their Rue de la Grosse-Tour. But they did not remain there long. Madame du Châtelet was called to Paris, and she took her philosopher with her, as well as her mathematician, Koenig, who followed her everywhere.

In the month of September of that year, 1739, the Parisian editor Prault published a collection of fugitive pieces, at the head of which figured an unpublished fragment of the "Histoire du Siècle de Louis XIV.," by Voltaire. The book was seized at the publishing office and the publisher condemned to pay a fine of five hundred livres and to shut up his house. Voltaire, fearing to be included in the pursuit, retired in all haste to the Château de Cirey.

Madame du Châtelet, seeking to attract Voltaire into the field of scientific studies, of exact sciences, sought to divert him from his love of poetry and his purely literary occupations. "When M. Voltaire is sick," she wrote, "he writes poetry." But Voltaire did not abandon himself to the wishes of his too learned friend. At that time he wrote:

"I love all the nine (the Muses). One should seek, as much as possible, to derive enjoyment from so many fair ones."

Voltaire has also painted Madame du Châtelet in her metamorphosis from the worldly into the scientific woman:

" But as the evening shades come on,
　Adown from her aphelion
　Our astronomic Emilie,
　Her hands with ink black as can be,
　And apron on, returns to me.
　To compasses she bids adieu,
　To reckonings, telescope;
　Her charms she now takes up anew:
　Those flowers beneath her steps that ope,
　Up to her toilet take with speed,
　And play for her upon thy reed
　Those melodies to love so dear,
　And which poor Newton did not hear."

In the month of December, 1739, we find him again, with the marchioness, in Brussels. The 10th of January, 1740, the Prince Royal had written him a letter made up of prose and verse, characterizing the Cardinal de Fleury as an old ungrateful priest, and which begins thus :

" For making France illustrious
　A thankless old priest banishes
　Thee from thy home, O princely bard !
　Old age makes him ridiculous;
　It is the way one punishes,
　But not that men reward."

Voltaire, very sensitive to the disagreeable results of Prault's publication, writes from Brussels to the Count d'Argental in February, 1740 :

" I intend to remain a long time in this country. I love the French, but hate persecution. I am indignant at being treated as I am."

And to the Marquess of Argenson, the 21st of May :

" The suit of Madame du Châtelet does not progress much. I must prepare myself to remain here long. I am with her; I am sheltered from persecution, and yet I regret you," etc.

Voltaire did not flatter the city of Brussels in 1740 any more than in 1739:

"I have not yet had the consolation of seeing my works correctly published," he writes to Frederick. "I could profit by my residence in Brussels to make a new edition [the 'Elements' are here alluded to], but Brussels is the abode of ignorance. There is not in it a printer, not an engraver, not a man of letters, and without Madame du Châtelet I could not converse of literature here. Moreover, this country is a country of servility. It has a papal nuncio and no Frederick."

In the course of January, 1740, the author of "Manon l'Escaut," the Abbé Prévost, had addressed a curious letter to Voltaire, in which he calls himself his most passionate admirer, and proposes becoming his liegeman to answer to the mob of pamphleteers bent on tarnishing his fame. Then, passing without other transition from his offer to the quest of services, he exposes to him his pressing need of twelve thousand livres, of which the lack causes him to be besieged by his creditors even into his very hotel. "Out of one thousand opulent persons with whom I pass my life, I wish to die if I know one of whom I have the hardihood to ask this sum, and of whom I feel sure of obtaining it."

Voltaire only answered the Abbé Prévost from Brussels in June, 1740. He begins by declaring himself highly flattered to be lauded by him, but that the motive which prevented the great Condé from writing his memoirs also stops him short, seeing that, like him, he would be obliged to bring on

the stage in a disagreeable manner a large number
of persons of a notorious ingratitude toward him, to
begin with the Abbé Desfontains, who owes him
his life, and who has rewarded him by every kind of
insult and pamphlet.

"Far from seeking to publish the shame of men
of letters," adds Voltaire, "I only seek to cover it
up.   There is a writer (like La Jonchère) who wrote
me one day, 'Here is, sir, a libel I have written
against you. If you will send me one hundred
crowns it will not appear.' I informed him that one
hundred crowns were too small a matter; that his
libel should be worth to him at least one hundred
pistoles, and that he should publish it. I would
never end with similar anecdotes, but they-paint
humanity in too ugly colors, and I prefer to forget
them."

Voltaire terminated his letter by informing the
Abbé Prevost that he intended sending him very
shortly the twelve thousand livres which he needed,
although in Brussels he was far from playing the
part of a farmer-general and living in opulence.   In
reality, it was an amiable turn for a refusal.

Some months after having received that answer
from Voltaire, the Abbé Prévost was himself obliged
to take refuge in Brussels, after having been accused
of collaborating in a secret gazette which circulated
in Paris.

"For some time, reported a member of the "Me-
moires Secrets de la Republique des Lettres," a
one-horse gazette filled with scandalous chronicles
has been circulated.   The delivering agents have
been arrested and put in jail; one of them has
denounced the Abbé Prévost. In consequence, the

Abbe Prévost has received the order of leaving the realm, and he started this morning for Brussels."

The fate of pamphleteers had nothing very pleasant in the last century. They were not in security, even when abroad. Voltaire informs us that Henri Dubourg, a French publicist, was carried away, in Frankfort, by an officer in the French army, and taken to the Mont-Saint-Michel, where he died in a cage. That pamphleteer hid under the pseudonym of Dubourg his real name of Victor de la Castaigne. He belonged to a family in the south of France.

It does not appear that the Abbé Prévost remained long in Brussels. He saw Voltaire there, after which he went to Holland, where he published several novels before going on to London. He took with him to the capital of Great Britain a young Holland woman who was passionately fond of him, and who would absolutely follow him in his new retreat. The poor Abbé Prévost, whom ill luck and women pursued all his life, returned to France only to meet a tragic end. While crossing the forest of Chantilly, he fell struck with apoplexy. Two passers-by raised him up and carried him to the house of a village priest. He gave no sign of life. To ascertain whether he was alive or dead, an ignorant surgeon gave him a vigorous and mortal thrust of the lancet, which made him open his eyes. The Abbe Prévost lived a few minutes more—long enough to see himself murdered by that surgeon.

VII.

Frederick had ascended the throne of Prussia in the month of June, 1740. Once king, he altered his views upon the advisability of publishing the refutation of Machiavel. He had ordered Voltaire to have it printed at the Hague, but he requested him to stop the impression of the "Anti-Machiavel;" of which Voltaire would say jocosely that the King of Prussia spit in the dish in order to disgust the rest.

Voltaire flies to the Hague, but the publisher, Van Durel, did not consent to give up the manuscript of the "Anti-Machiavel," and was resolved on printing it *nolens volens*, in spite of Voltaire, who returned to Brussels defeated by the Dutch printer.

Notwithstanding the King of Prussia burned with the desire to see Voltaire, the philosopher remained for some time deaf to the invitations of the king, as is attested by this letter of the 28th of June, 1740, addressed to M. de Cideville:

"Withal, I remain in Brussels, and the best king upon the earth, his merits and his glory, will not draw me for one moment away from Emilie. Kings, even this one, must come only after friends."

But, Frederick having used new persuasions, Voltaire proposes to him to visit him in company with his Emilie, Madame du Châtelet; to which the King of Prussia answers:

"I shall write to Madame du Châtelet in accordance with your desire. To speak frankly to you concerning her voyage, it is Voltaire, it is you, my friend, whom I desire to see; and the divine Emilie, with all her divinity, is but the accessory of Apollo Newtonized."

Two days later comes another ironical letter from the king :

"If it needs be that Emilie accompany Apollo, I consent. But if I can see you alone, I prefer this last. I would be too dazzled, I could not bear so much splendor at once; I would need Moses' veil to temper the united rays of your divinities."

But suddenly all is changed. The King of Prussia has projected a voyage to the Netherlands, which he will extend to Anvers and Brussels. The colony of Grosse-Tour street is upside down. Voltaire writes to Frederick that he shall expect to offer him the hospitality of his modest retreat, and that Madame du Châtelet has already prepared his apartments.

"If it became true," adds he, "that your humanity should pass through Brussels, I implore her to bring me English drops, for I shall faint."

"It will be the most charming day of my life," answers Frederick. "I believe I shall not survive; but at least one could not choose a more agreeable manner of death."

Unfortunately, a fever made a change in the traveling arrangements of the king. On the 6th of September, 1740, he wrote to Voltaire from Wessel to beg him to come and meet him at Cleves :

"My dear Voltaire, I must, say what I will, give up to the fever, which is more tenacious than a Jansenist; and, however greatly I desired to go to Anvers and Brussels, I do not find myself in the condition to undertake such a voyage without risk. I would ask you, then, if the road from Brussels to

Cleves would seem too long for you to join me there? Let us defraud the fever, my dear Voltaire, and may I at least have the pleasure of embracing you. Be good enough to present to the Marchioness my excuses for being deprived of the satisfaction of seeing her in Brussels. Sunday next I shall be in a little place near by Cleves, where I shall be able to possess you really at my ease."

. The meeting of the two illustrious friends took place on the 11th of September, 1740, in the castle of Moyland, near Cleves. It was a charming one. The presence of Voltaire, face to face with whom he found himself for the first time, gave such a delight to the king that his fever was checked by it so much that he arose and appeared at supper, where literature and philosophy were discussed while flowed the champagne, less effervescent than Voltaire's wit. Frederick II. was delighted with the opportunity of at last conversing with the wittiest man of his time, the first of thinking beings. He cried out, like a jealous lover, "How happy is Emilie in possessing him!" To which the marchioness seemed to give an answer when she wrote from Brussels to Maupertuis, bitterly complaining to him of the prolonged absence of Voltaire:

"I hope the King of Prussia," said she, "will soon send me back somebody with whom I intend to spend my life, and whom I only lent him for a few days."

Madame du Châtelet deemed it monstrous to leave a woman to go and meet a sovereign.

Pulled about between the marchioness and that king, Voltaire leaned to Frederick's side and competed with him in amiabilities and coquetries. Hav-

ing left him to go to the Hague to correct the proof-
sheets of the "Anti-Machiavel," he had the cruelty
of not returning to Brussels, where waited the dis-
appointed Madame du Châtelet. He entered the
Prussian realm under the jocular name of Don Qui-
xote, and rejoined Frederick at Remusberg.

The time passed by Voltaire at Remusberg was a
series of festivals, of merry banquets, a concert of
mutual flatteries and admiration. However, Voltaire remembers the divine Emilie. The time for
leaving Prussia has arrived. But Frederick still
wants to detain the first of thinking beings. Voltaire sends him this last parting pastoral:

"In spite of your great worth, in spite of all your charms,
       My soul is discontented yet.
       No! no! you are but a coquette,
Who subjugates our hearts and yet would flee our arms."

Frederick, defeated in his endeavor to detain Voltaire at his court and to separate him from Emilie,
retorted:

"My heart doth fully know the value of your charms;
     But do not deem it could thus be contented yet.
     Ah, traitor! you leave me, and that for a coquette;
I *ne'er* could flee thy arms."

After visiting Berlin to pay his court to the queen-
mother and the sisters of the king, Voltaire started
on his way to rejoin the "coquette" Emilie, as she
was called by her rival, the King of Prussia.

The marchioness, who, with feminine tact, had
felt a personal enemy in Frederick, and who at heart
was wounded at not having been invited by him,
could not forgive Voltaire for having preferred a

king to her, and for having left her alone in Brussels with Koenig, his physique and intellect, and her interminable lawsuit.

Voltaire developed all the amiability of his mind, and succeeded in obtaining forgiveness for his prolonged absence, so that he wrote to the Count of Argental, "Never has Madame du Châtelet been more superior to kings."

And, on her side, Madame du Châtelet informs the Count of Argental that "at last he [Voltaire] has arrived. All our sorrows are at an end, and he swears to me they are indeed at an end forever. The King of Prussia is much astonished to find that one can leave him to go to Brussels. He asked three days' grace; but it was refused him. He has no conception of certain attachments; it is to be hoped that it will but make his friendships stronger. He has left nothing undone to retain our friend, and I believe him to be in a fury against me; but I defy him to hate me more than I have hated him for two months past. Here is, you will allow, a merry rivalry."

And, in fact, the King of Prussia had for Voltaire one of those impassioned friendships which were seen in ancient Greece between men who chose one another, and which Frederick carried to the point of being jealous of Madame du Châtelet. At any rate, this duel between a king and a marchioness is of the greatest piquancy, and Madame du Châtelet goes to the very limits of irony when she writes, "He has no conception of certain attachments; it is to be hoped that it will but make him love his friends the more."

Voltaire, once more a *Bruxellois*, and reinstated in his Grosse-Tour street, to the great delight of the Marchioness, gave the last touch to his " Mahomet," which was played in Lille, in April, 1740, with the plaudits of an enthusiastic audience. The prelates of Lille themselves contributed to this success.

Perfectly quiet and sheltered from all persecution in Brussels, Voltaire worked at his tragedy of " Merope," when the lawsuit which had retained Madame du Châtelet in Brussels for such a long time called her back to Champagne to plead in the nearer jurisdiction of Cirey; after which it became necessary again to return to Brussels.

Voltaire accompanied his Emilie in all her judiciary peregrinations, and with her left the capital of Brabant in November, 1744, to go on to Cirey.

From Cirey, Voltaire returned with his friend to Paris, which he called the " Capital of trifles," whilst he recognized all it had that was great and beautiful. His " Brutus " met with a season of renewed and lively success. All the clerical hounds, the Desfontaines and the Frerons, were let loose against this republican piece. Voltaire faced his enemies, ridiculing them, piercing them with his arrows, with his darts of sarcasm. Against his sworn enemy, Freron, he launched the following taunt, imitated from the " Anthologic :"

> " In yonder vale (I do not lie)
> A viper stung poor Jean Freron.
> What think you happened thereupon?
> It was the snake that had to die."

To the Abbe Couet, high-vicar of the Cardinal of Noailles, who had addressed him his Grace's man-

date, he retorted by sending one of his tragedies,
"Marianne," with this quatrain :

> " Thy gracious mandate came to me;
> I send thee back a tragedy.
> Thus, thou for me, and I for thee,
> Do we both play the comedy."

It is with enthusiasm that Goldsmith speaks of
Voltaire, whom he saw at that time in a soiree of
the Parisian society, where the conversation turned
upon the merits of English literature. Fontenelle,
being but little acquainted with it, did not appreciate it. Diderot contradicted him. But Voltaire
presented its claims with a grace and a reality that
charmed the author of the "Vicar of Wakefield."

VIII.

Soon another storm broke out over the head of
Voltaire, who was, however, accustomed to these
thunderbolts. One of his letters to the King of
Prussia had been intercepted, and copies of it had
been circulated.

"Do you know the last thing out?" wrote the
president Henault to Madame du Deffand. "It is a
letter of Voltaire to the King of Prussia, the most
foolish that could be imagined. He tells him he has
done well to conclude peace, that the half of Paris
approves him, that he has only gotten ahead of the
cardinal, that he must busy himself now only with
recalling pleasures, those children of the arts, the
opera, comedy, etc. Madame de Mailly breathes
only fire and revenge, and demands an exemplary
punishment. It is not known what will come of it,

and it is feared the end will be a decampment to Brussels."

All the enemies of Voltaire, eagerly seizing upon this new weapon, circumvented the favorite, Madame de Mailly, and strove to make Voltaire appear a traitor to his country. The letter in question was believed to have been surrendered by a post-carrier of Brussels, who had been bought over by the police of the French minister.

"It is neither God nor devil," Frederick wrote to him, "but, indeed, a miserable Brussels clerk who opened and copied your letter and has sent it to Paris and everywhere."

But Voltaire, better informed, replied later, from Brussels, exonerating the post-service of that city:

"I know for a certainty that it is not a Brussels clerk who opened the letter which has become my box of Pandora. The whole of that fine exploit came off in Paris in the time of a crisis, and it is a clerk of the person whom your majesty suspects (the Cardinal Fleury) who has done all this evil."

Voltaire sent protestations of love for his country to different persons, notably to the Cardinal Fleury and to the favorite, Madame du Mailly, claiming to be a good citizen, profoundly attached to his country, and that his relations with the King of Prussia had no character hostile to France, concluding that if he had indeed written the falsified letter as they circulated it, it would deserve indignation. However—we must say it—the letter was certainly from him. It was a blunder.

Before his plausible affirmations the balloon emptied itself. But, after having passed at the bar on account of patriotism, the bigot party charged him

with having ridiculed the Christian religion and
having exposed Christ to derision under the name
of "Mahomet," a tragedy played at the Theater
Français, the 20th of August, 1742.

More acute than the clergy of Lille, the Parisian
clergy saw plainly that by placing "Mahomet" on
the stage the author had aimed at Christ, and especially at fanaticism, which, besides, was the secondary title of the piece: "Mahomet ou le Fanatisme."
Some doctors of the Sorbonne judged that "Mahomet" was a cutting satire upon the Christian religion.
An Englishman had judged the piece in the same
way.

"Voltaire," wrote Chesterfield to Crebillon, Jr.,
"recited before me last year, in Brussels, several extracts from his 'Mahomet,' where I found very fine
lines and some thoughts more brilliant than just;
but I saw at once that Jesus Christ was aimed at
under the character of Mahomet, and I was surprised
they had failed to perceive it in Lille."

The representation of "Mahomet" in Paris produced an incredible sensation. The whole tribe of
the Desfontaines and Frerons, all the clerical pack,
howled against the piece. The main body and rear-
guard of the genus bigot rose and fulminated—even
the Jansenists and the Convulsionnaires (for it was
the happy time of the sinister extravagancies of the
cemetery of St. Medard), and that so well that the
Cardinal of Fleury entreated Voltaire to withdraw
his tragedy to put an end to scandal.

"Since I am now the victim of the Jansenists,"
wrote Voltaire to the Count of Argental, "I shall
dedicate 'Mahomet' to the pope, and I expect

to become bishop *in partibus infidelium*, seeing that is my true diocese."

Sure enough, three years later, Voltaire kept his word and sent to Benoit XIV. his tragedy, with a Latin distich to place below his portrait, and wrote him, while dedicating " Mahomet " to him:

" May your holiness deign to allow me to place at -your feet book and author. I dare ask your benediction for the one and protection for the other. It is with these sentiments of a profound veneration that I prostrate myself before you and kiss your sacred feet."

Benoit XIV. answers his " dear son Voltaire," while sending him, in a brief of felicitation, his greeting and apostolic benediction. He thanked him for his distich, accepted the dedication of " Mahomet," and became the champion of the author, who, thanks to the brief of the pope, was able again to place his piece upon the stage in 1745.

The Paris clergy spread the rumor that the pope had fallen into a ridiculous trap; but Benoit XIV. knew what he was about. It pleased him to show his amiable Atticism to protect such a genius as Voltaire; and, besides, he would have blushed to play the part of an ignorant friar, always fulminating, always wrathful, which the sovereign pontiffs of the nineteenth century have played in the name of a Catholicism as narrow as inflexible. In the eighteenth century everybody had wit—even the popes!

Let us return to Paris, to the storm raised by the first representations of " Mahomet." Seeing it would not calm down, Voltaire, according to his usual prudence, "pulled up stakes," and regained, with his friend, on the 25th of August, 1742, his secure asy-

lum, Brussels, whence he started again on the 2d of
September to answer the pressing call of the King
of Prussia, who was then at Aix. The interview
was very short this time. Voltaire remained only
three days with Frederick.

"He offers me a good house in Berlin and a fine
estate," says Voltaire, "but I prefer still my second
story in Madame du Châtelet's house. He insures
me his favor and the preservation of my liberty, and
I run to Paris to my bondage and to persecution."

Yet the two friends had never more congratulated
or burnt more incense for one another. For the
King of Prussia, Voltaire was the wisest, the most
illustrious, the most virtuous of men. As for Voltaire, he wrote to this king, the Alexander and the
Solomon of the North, in a dithyrambic tone, wherein
a shade of irony peers out:

"Oh, most extraordinary of men who win battles,
who take provinces, who make peace, who make
poetry and music, the whole of which so pleasantly
and gayly!"

Voltaire, who had never better and more quietly
worked than in Belgium, acquires more genial appreciation of Brussels. He writes to the Count of Argental:

"We have led in Brussels a retired life, which is
much to my taste. I found few men, but many
books. I worked without cessation."

To Madame de Champbonin:

"We live in Brussels as in Cirey. We see few
people. We study during the day; we sup gayly.
We take our coffee and milk on the morrow of a
good supper. I am sick sometimes, but very con-

tented with my lot, and feeling no lack but that of your presence."

And to Thiérot :

"Madame du Châtelet still continues her miserable chicanery war here. For me, I am subjected to all the tricks of the printers."

To prevent the closing of the doors of France against him, Voltaire writes from Brussels to the Cardinal Minister de Fleury to render account of his interview with Frederick. He writes him that the king is grieved and piqued by the hostility of France, towards which his tastes attract him. He would not be much adverse to contracting an alliance with his government. He had asked information touching the financial resources of France. Voltaire had answered him that they were immense, etc. It is evident that Voltaire intentionally exaggerates the good dispositions of the King of Prussia for his country, and that he gives court holy water to the Cardinal.

In that same year, 1742, died Rousseau. A subscription for the publication of his works was made. When sending his contribution, Voltaire, forgetting the polemics of old, wrote what follows to M. Segui:

"It appeared as if destiny, in leading me to the city (Brussels) where the illustrious and unhappy Rousseau has ended his life, reserved for me a reconciliation with him. His talents, his misfortunes, and his death have smothered all resentment in my heart, and have left my eyes open to his merits alone."

In November, 1742, Voltaire left Brussels. On the 20th of February, 1743, he put his "Merope" on the stage in Paris. This tragedy met with a complete success. Voltaire was carried in triumph into the lodge of the Maréchale de Villars, and the young Duchess of Villars, urged by an enthusiastic public, was forced to kiss the author of " Merope," amid the plaudits of the whole audience.

Voltaire once more offered himself to the Academy. But its doors were still closed against him by the Minister Maurepas, at the head of a hostile faction. The King of Prussia strove to console Voltaire in this defeat by addressing him the following letter:

"I expected certainly to see Voltaire repelled whenever he appeared before an Areopagus of cross-and-miter Midases. Prevail upon yourself to learn to despise a nation which ignores the merit of the Belle-Isles and of the Voltaires. Come to a land where you are loved and bigotry is not."

Voltaire experienced another and quite as painful reverse. It was the Ministerial interdiction of his "Julius Cæsar," which was upon the eve of being brought out. Indignant at this arbitrary and vexing measure, Voltaire was about to leave France once more, when a diplomatic mission was proposed to this interdicted author, to this publicist so often pursued and exiled. The new Minister of War, the Count of Argenson, had had the idea of utilizing the friendship of Voltaire and Frederick to strive and obtain through it an alliance between France and Prussia. Frederick, at peace with all his enemies, had signed the treaty of Breslau, which greatly displeased the French, whose policy sought to cause him again to take up arms.

Although Voltaire saw all the difficulty of that delicate mission, the consequences of which might be the rupture of his good relations with Frederick, he accepted it to serve his country, which, according to his own expression, had so often treated him in a shameful manner. But he loved France, and blind enemies alone could have accused him of a lack of patriotism, without succeeding in basing their calumnies upon any real fact.

Madame du Châtelet, who had not been initiated into the secret of the diplomatic mission, wrote at that time:

"He has gone to Holland, whence he will probably go to Prussia, which is what I fear above all, for the King of Prussia is a dangerous rival for me. At the end of July I shall go to Brussels, where he has promised to meet me again."

IX.

Voltaire went on to the Hague in the course of the month of June, 1743, in order to spy out the attitude of the Hollanders and the military forces of England in that country. He was lodged in the palace of the old court property of the King of Prussia, whom he soon rejoined in Berlin. There Voltaire thought of his mission, and undertook to win over Frederick, who was rather surprised and displeased to see his philosopher transformed into a French diplomat. However, he did not discourage him at first, and listened to him with a careless ear. Voltaire played his part seriously. To compel Frederick to make him some categoric answer, he would send him his political observations upon a sheet of paper of which a large margin was left blank. But Frederick replied by jests, by small rhymes and pleasantries. By the side of Voltaire's observation that the friends of Austria burned to open the campaign in Silesia, Frederick put on the margin the burden of an old comic song, running something thus :

"Ah! we will be on hand for the lads—fee dle dee—
In the fashion of old Yankee doodle dandee—
You shall see!"*

The most curious phase of this diplomatic comedy was that at the very moment when Voltaire strove to bring the courts of Prussia and France together,

* On les y recevra, biribi,
A la façon de barbari,
Mon ami.

Frederick sought to compromise him with the Court of Versailles.

"I would embroil him forever with France," said the King of Prussia. "That would be the way to have him at Berlin."

And to accomplish this aim Frederick caused the circulation in Versailles, under false covers, of satirical verses of Voltaire upon the court, upon the ministers, and even some fragments of the "Pucelle" which had escaped Emilie's scrutiny.

The progress of this little plot of the King of Prussia was divulged and stopped by some indiscretion. Voltaire felt much hurt by it. "He thought to succeed," he has written, "by ruining me in France." After considerable moping, a reconciliation took place, nevertheless, and Voltaire familiarly said to Frederick, "Never play me any more tricks!" Then he spoke seriously of his mission to him, and begged the king to charge him with some mission to the court of Versailles.

Frederick, in his turn, took up a serious tone. He said to him that he had no connection with France and no answer to make, having received no direct application. "The only mission which I can give you for France is to counsel her to act more wisely than she has done up to the present."

Voltaire perceived some change had come in his relations with Frederick. "He scented the spy," he has himself said. Voltaire, as a skillful diplomat, alternated his mission by saying that, after all, he had only been charged with fomenting sentiments of concord between the two monarchs. The cloud passed over.

Nevertheless, Voltaire held his ground. As Fred-

erick was about to leave Berlin to make a review of
the little principalities of Germany to test and sound
them in view to the eventualities of the future, Voltaire asked to go along, which was granted him.
At Bayreuth, Frederick left our philosopher-diplomat with his sister the Margravine, and went on his
way.

Voltaire remained nearly a month in Bayreuth, in
Brunswick, in Anspach, in the midst of homages, of
feasts, of a veritable enchantment. Frederick's sisters, the Margravine of Bayreuth and the Princess
Ulrich, loved letters and men of letters as well as
their brother. Voltaire, charmed with his reception,
addressed gallant verses and madrigals to the princesses, who, on their side, were delighted with his
wit and jollity.

Here is a bouquet to Chloris which Voltaire addressed to the Princess Ulrich, and which is too
charming for us to fail in culling it from among his
witty poetical blossoms :

> " 'Tis often that a grain of truth
>   Is mingled with the coarsest lies:
>   This night, in dreams, I saw, forsooth,
>   Myself to rank of kings arise.
>
> Ah! princess, I loved thee—to thee my flame avowed.—
> I waked. The gods in part to keep my dream allowed;
>   I only lost the crown, the thing I did not prize."

"It is a celestial voyage, during which I pass from
planet to planet," has said Voltaire about his agreeable excursion among the little German principalities.

"He is absolutely intoxicated, he has gone mad
with the German courts," wrote Madame du Châtelet, who during all this time uttered the cries of a

forsaken Ariadne. "He remained fifteen days at Bayreuth without the king. He was three weeks without writing me. For two months past I learn of his whereabouts by the embassadors and the gazettes. You will easily understand how much I am to be pitied. But, in spite of myself, I cannot tear away from him. Notwithstanding all I suffer, I am well convinced that the one who loves the most is the happiest, after all."

She writes again from Paris to the Count of Argental, on the 23d of November, 1743, a melancholy letter, in which is found this passage:

"I return to Brussels, there to end a life in which I have had more happiness than sorrow, and which is terminating at a time when I could no longer bear it."

At last Voltaire, after having torn himself away from the delights of the little German courts, returned to Berlin to take his leave of the king, who gave to the philosopher-diplomat, it appears, some good word for the court of Versailles. Then he rejoined Madame du Châtelet in Brussels in the last days of October, 1743. But he could only grant her a few hours. Was he not obliged to go to Versailles and render account of his mission? As it had produced no immediate results, he received no thanks for it. The favorite, Madame de Châteauroux, was piqued at not having been consulted concerning the sending of the philosopher to Prussia. And yet, to use a celebrated phrase, the fault did not lie with Voltaire. The King of Prussia, exposed to the hatred of England and to the grudges of the Queen of Holland, would have naturally inclined to a French alliance could he have placed any dependence upon

a court abandoned to Jesuits and favorites, upon a
king whose policy was as vacillating as his character.

The following year, however, the King of Prussia
decided for a favorable attitude towards France.
Voltaire has himself established the efficacy of his
mission and of the service he had rendered to his
country by the following:

"I gave to the court of Versailles the hopes given
me at Berlin. They were not fallacious, and the
following spring the King of Prussia did, in fact
make a new treaty with the King of France. He
invaded Bohemia with a hundred thousand men
while the Austrians were in Alsace."

Thus repelled, and having reaped ingratitude as a
reward for his mission and his efforts, the ubiquist
and Wandering Jew Voltaire, to follow whom puts
one out of breath, returns to Brussels, on the 1st of
February, 1744. He remained there for some time
quiet and laborious, at the hearth of the divine Emilie. His printed correspondence contains but one
letter dated from Brussels, the 2d of February of
that same year, 1744, and addressed to the Count of
Argental. Here follows a fragment of it:

"The Hollanders do not declare themselves. The
King of England will bear all the burden, which is
somewhat heavy. The Hanoverians who are camp-
ing at the gates of Brussels publicly say they are
led to slaughter, and feel quite sorry for the trip. I
saw the Flemish troops, ragged and badly paid.
Eleven months' pay is actually due the officers.
Well, well! sons of France, rejoice!"

M. Desnoireterres thinks that Voltaire must have
written several letters from Brussels at this period,

and that they must have been lost by a deplorable mischance.

About this time, the king of Prussia addressed him, at Brussels, a missive terminating in this pleasant manner :

"Adieu, admirable historian, great poet, charming author of the 'Pucelle,' that invisible and sad prisoner of Circe (the Moergrave of Bayreuth) ; adieu to the lover of Valori's cook, of Madame de Châtelet, and of my sister."

From Brussels Voltaire went to the castle of Cirey, where the tedious suit of Madame du Châtelet was at last terminated by a transaction advantageous to her.

X.

At the end of the year 1744 Voltaire again appears in Paris. Influenced by Madame du Châtelet, who still feared to see the king of Prussia take back his prey, and above all, by the necessity of defending himself against his numerous enemies, he becomes a courtier. He obtains his *entrées* at Versailles, Fontainebleau, and Sceaux. His ballet-comedy, "*la Princesse de Navarre,*" is represented in Versailles, at the celebration of the dauphin's marriage with the infanta of Spain. Some witty madrigals, some grains of incense burnt in honor of the favorite, Mme. de Pompadour, gain for him the protection of that mistress of Louis XV., to whom he addressed flatteries in rhymes, and madrigals like the following :

> Ah ! Pompadour, thy brush divine,
> Alone thy beauty should retrace,
> Thus art could never more combine
> A fairer hand with fairer face.

Aided by the influence of the favorite, Voltaire enters the academy, becomes one of the Forty, is appointed historiographer of France, and in 1746 gentleman-at-ordinary with the king. Voltaire, as a courtier, dwindled, but at least his suppleness insured him a truce. He breathed for some time in Paris. As historiographer, he composed the "*Bataille de Fontenoy,*" which is not his best poem.

In the following stanza, Voltaire ridicules his experience as court poet, and the favors which buffooneries worthy of a traveling show had drawn down upon him :

My Henry, with the younger Zaire,
And my American Alzaire
Together gained me not a notice of the king ;
Ah ! many foes had I, with very little fame,
Yet a buffonery unworthy of a name
Has honors to me now brought on their fleetest wing.

Madame du Châtelet was ill at court, like her *alter ego*. She was of the *queen's play*, and one evening, in Fontainebleau, she lost in it a trifle of 80,000 francs. Voltaire, with his ordinary vivacity and ready tongue, having styled the lords of the *jeu de la reine* (queen's play), as audacious Greeks and swindlers, found it necessary to disappear with Emilie and to seek refuge with the duchess of Maine, in her castle of Sceaux.

Behind the curtains and blinds of the duchess, Voltaire composed the greater part of his novels and tales. On her side, Madame du Châtelet played the comedy in Sceaux and in Anet. Emilie was tremendously applauded, while acting with universal satisfaction, Mademoiselle de la Cochonnière (pig-sty) in the *Count de Boursoufflé* (Count of High-Swell), of Voltaire. His charming comedy, "Nanine," was also enthusiastically received by the aristocratic audience.

Voltaire, ever emerging again after his successive divings, returned to Paris and addressed the Pompadour with a madrigal which so delighted the favorite that she communicated it to all her suite. Unfortunately the abandoned queen, Mary Leczinska, who was none the less the queen, was piqued at this and considered in the light of a public insult that madrigal in which Voltaire associated the fates of the Pompadour and of Louis XV. for eternity. The queen demanded Voltaire's exile, and Louis XV. signed it.

Decidedly madrigals were not more successful in' protecting the poet-philosopher from persecution than his cutting epigrams.

Voltaire withdrew with Emilie to the castle of Cirey. Some time after, the châtelaine of the manor having received from the king of Poland, Stanislas, that living *roi d' Yvetot* (character of one of the the immortal Béranger's best songs ; a jolly village king), a graceful and amiable imitation, to visit his court of Lunéville (in Lorraine), Voltaire, equally invited, accompanied her there.

Being now, to use his expression, only a tributary planet of the divine Emilie, he followed her to the diminutive court in Lorraine. It was the home of pleasure, of comedy in all its styles, where shone the marchioness of Boufflers, mistress of Stanislas, and the marquess of St. Lambert, author of the " Seasons " and of the " Ode to Chloe." Sorry poet and sorry man, indeed, he had in him the two seductive poetical charms, the two enchantments of life, youth and passion.

Voltaire had left Lunéville to go to Paris, in order to oversee the rehearsals of " Sémiramis. In 1749, he resorted to Commercy (in Lorraine, near Nancy). It was there he became apprised of the relations between Madame du Châtelet and St. Lambert.

A rupture was threatened. But the Marchioness

knew well what reliance she could place in the
staunch friendship of Voltaire. That disinterested
and most devoted man forgave the weakness of the
divine Emilie.

M. Blaze de Bury has said in excellent terms in
the *Revue des Deux Mondes:*

"Pitiless for the tyrannies, the defender of Calais
and Sirven ever had tender bowels for his fellow-
beings; even toward the women who deceived him,
he was kind and clement."

How could he have been otherwise than clement
toward women, the man who said, "Women are the
most precious gifts of nature to men," and who
ceaselessly repeated, "Woe to callous hearts!"

But Madame du Châtelet neared her end. Becoming pregnant, she goes to Luneville, where she gives
birth to a daughter.

Three days after her delivery, the Marchioness
having committed the imprudence of drinking a
glass of orgeat, was carried off by the fever in one
night. Voltaire was inconsolable.

Sometimes a man of genius finds forgiveness before the world, but a superior woman rarely does.
The death of the Marchioness du Châtelet was
greeted with epigrams and venomous imputations at
the French and Prussian courts.

The inveterate enemy of Emilie, the king of
Prussia, did not fail to pass his table-companions a
cutting epitaph upon the deceased marchioness.

In France, Collé greeted her death in his journal
with this gross insult, which he took doubtless for a
witty stroke:

"I learn from Estioles that Madame du Châtelet
died in child-birth. It is to be hoped it will be the

last time she will give herself airs. To die at child-
birth at her age, is to affect singularity ; it shows a
pretention of doing nothing like other folks."

By the side of these sad posthumous retaliations, of
these sepulchral satires, it is a happiness to be able
to quote the lines of Voltaire, written below her portrait, and which reproduced quite faithfully, although
not without somewhat embellishing, her physiognomy :

> " The world has lost thee, noble Emilie,
> Who lovedst art and truth and pleasures free.
> The gods who did bestow their soul on thee,
> Withheld no gift but immortality."

But more intensely than in these lines does the
profound sorrow inflicted to the poet by the loss of
his companion of so many years appear in this letter
to the court of Argental :

" I have lost the half of myself, a soul for whom
mine was made, a friend of twenty years whom I
saw born. The most tender father loves not otherwise his only daughter. I love again to find her
memory everywhere ; I love to speak to her husband, to her son."

XI.

Voltaire left Cirey, now deserted by the goddess, and reëntered the Parisian arena toward the month of October, 1749. He renewed the struggle with ardor, desiring to reduce to their just value the fame and tragedies of Crebillon over which the public were going mad. At the beginning of the year 1750, Voltaire had his "Oreste" played at the *Théâtre Francais*. Although he cried from his loge to partisans of Crebillon in a cabal against his piece : "Applaud, barbarians, that is Sophocles himself. . .," the tragedy had but a moderate success. Voltaire did not lose courage. In Sceana, and upon a stage improvised in his mansion in Traversiere street, he brought out "Alzaire" and "Catiline" (the Rescue of Rome), admirably creating in this last piece the role of Cicero. Both public and success answered to his expectations.

As long as Voltaire remained on the domain of comedy, he did not experience any violent opposition, but as soon as his pen could freely treat some historical or philosophical theme, the alarm was taken and he was threatened. Thus he raised new troubles for himself by coming out as the advocate of the equality of taxation in the *Voix du sage et du peuple* (the Voice of the Sage and of the People), as well as the apologist of the *Esprit des Lois* (a work of Montesquieu), and of Montesquieu in his

Remerciement sincère à un homme charitable, or
Sincere Thanks to a Charitable Man.

The favor of Petticoat II. (Madame de Pompadour), was a precious preservative against the fury
of his foes. Voltaire, feverish, tempestuous as he
was, with his mind in constant ebullition, made
a strange courtier, who, with his velvet paw scratched
nevertheless the hand he caressed. It was thus he
brought upon himself the disfavor of his protectress
by correcting her in the midst of a banquet upon the
word *grassonillette* (plumpy), used by her about a
very fine quail :

> I softly whisper it, my fair *Pompadourette*,
> But *plumpy* seems to me not quite good etiquette.

To say, *I softly whisper it*, was not quite strictly
exact, since the guests could all hear this somewhat
free correction.

The Pompadour felt wounded, and withdrew from
the philosopher the hand which had protected him.
As for Louis XV., he cordially detested Voltaire,
and to such a degree that some years previous, after
the representation of the "Temple of Glory," written for him by his historiographer, as Voltaire said
to him at the end of the piece, " Is Trajan satisfied ?"
the king passed on in disdain, and preserved an
insulting silence.

Wearied with thus being butted against at every
turn, thrown from Charybdis to Scylla in that
empty court where, to live in peace, it would have
been necessary to be as worthless as a courtier, as
dumb as Louis XV., Voltaire having the consciousness of his mission, and unwilling to see his genius
stultified, decided to accept the propositions of the

king of Prussia, who was again calling him to
Berlin, offering him a pension of £20,000 with the
post of chamberlain.

Lord Chesterfield was much astonished by this
predilection of Voltaire for Prussia.

"I am assured," he wrote, "that Voltaire has
definitively established himself in Berlin. Do explain me the motive of such an emigration."

But the secret of the enigma was very easy to
unravel. Voltaire was seeking abroad in Berlin the
healthful atmosphere and the freedom necessary to
the thinker, the author, and which were lacking to
him in France.

"It is abroad," he has said, "that I must think
and write for France."

At home, indeed, he had but the choice between
the Bastille or unmanly abdication at the court of
Louis, between the asphyxia of incarceration or of
submission. Rejecting these two extremities, Voltaire retired this time into voluntary exile. He went
to Prussia, leaving Paris on the 18th of June, 1756,
and only returning to die in 1778.

On the 2d of July he passed through Cleves, having gone by way of Flanders, and visited the battle-
fields of Fontenay, Rancourt, and Lawfeld.

The cowardly and ferocious pack of courtiers and
literary pigmies, whom Voltaire so wittily called
arlequins anthropophayes, criticised his flight to
Prussia. The king and Madame de Pompadour
even became riled at seeing the Alexander of the
North thus enticing away from them the most illustrious minds of France. But who was to blame?

"It is ludicrous," wrote Voltaire to his niece,
Madame Denis, to see these very literary men of

Paris, who would have *exterminated* me but a year ago, actually clamoring now against my retirement, and calling it desertion. It seems as if they regretted having lost their victim. . . ."

The peace of Aix la Chapelle had given some leisure to Frederick. He used it to indulge in literary taste and Freethinking views in his court at Berlin, which he had made a center of science and philosophy in the eighteenth century, thus realizing the words he had uttered some years previous, saying, " I want my capital to become the asylum of great men."

In Berlin congregated poets, authors, and savants, among whom Maupertuis, La Mettrie, d'Argens, Chasot, Algaroti, Polnitz, Lord Tirconnel, and others. Voltaire went to complete the brilliant pleiad, of which it might have been said :

" 'Tis from the north to-day that light to us doth shine."

Upon his arrival at Berlin, Voltaire writes, in his enthusiasm :

" One hundred and fifty thousand victorious soldiers, no prosecuting attorneys (as in Paris), opera, comedy, poetry, a hero, philosopher, and poet, grandeur, and grace, grenadiers and the muses, bugles and violins, Platonic repasts, society, and liberty, who could believe it ? Yet all this is real."

On his side the king of Prussia felt proud at securing Voltaire to his court, at having torn him away from France, and he said in a session of his academy :

" I shall not spread my conquests toward France. I have taken Voltaire from France, that is worth more than a province."

It was a perpetual feast, an incessant delight. In

the brilliant suppers of Potsdam and of Sans-Souci, all subjects were treated with the most entire freedom.

"Never in any place in the world" says Voltaire, "have all the superstitions of men been discussed with more liberty, and never were they treated with more sarcasm, jest, and contempt. God was respected, but all who had deceived men in his name were anything else but spared."

XII.

Three years sufficed to overshadow and mar this brilliant tableau of philosophical life in Prussia. Sad as it may be, it is nevertheless true that philosophers are only men, and therefore addicted to many of the foibles of ordinary mortals.

While elaborating his own works, and putting the finishing touches to his *Siecle de Louis XIV.*, Voltaire retouched oftimes the somewhat incorrect although ever witty and pointed lucubrations of Frederick. The poet loved to style himself as the washerman and dyer of the Prussian king. He probably allowed some indiscreet remarks of the kind to escape him before Frederick, whom in familiar moments he playfully called *Madame Alcine.*

Besides, in the scientific quarrel between Maupertuis and Kœnig, Voltaire had taken sides with the latter in opposition to the king who, so to speak, worshiped Maupertuis. Jealous of Voltaire's superiority and influence, Maupertuis saw his advantage. He spread a report that Voltaire had derided the king's pretensions to talent, and that when criticising the verses Frederick took delight in writing against the *beloved* Louis XV., he had said that the king could produce nothing of any merit. The accused was certainly prolific in epigrams. But he had never denied the king's talent, and the accusation was false.

Learning from what direction the blow had come, Voltaire published in Berlin an anonymous pamphlet filled with keen thrusts and biting sarcasms against Maupertuis. But Frederick, still taking part with his savant, had the executioner burn in the open street the *Diatribe of Doctor Akakia.*

This act on the part of the king irritated Voltaire. Life in Berlin, together with the despotic humor of Frederick, began to weigh upon our philosopher, who, loving freedom above all things, could never put on the regulation coat of the courtier without making it crack at every seam. He was willing to bow before freethinking monarchs while he fashioned them according to his own ideas, but he intended they should first respect his intellectual royalty. In a word, he was resolved they should deal with him as power with power. His bitterness and disappointment were expressed in the following letter, addressed to Madame Denis, in December, 1752:

"As I have not in the world fifty thousand *mustachios* at my service, I do not intend going to war. I am only thinking about deserting honorably, taking care of my health and forgetting this three years' dream.

"I see plainly they have squeezed the *orange;* I must take care now and save the *peel.* To amuse myself, I shall make a small lexicon for the use of kings. So, *My dear friend,* means you are more than indifferent to me. By *I will make you happy,* understand, I shall put up with you as long as I need you. *Sup with me this evening* signifies, I shall make sport of you this evening. What perplexes me is how to get out of this place."

Indeed it was not easy to break away from the

court of Prussia. Yet the day was not far distant
when Voltaire and Frederick, these two Athenians
of the eighteenth century, were to separate in ill-
humor. Bent on leaving, Voltaire returns to Frederick his cross and his key of Chamberlain. Frederick sends them back, inviting Voltaire to follow him
to Postdam. Voltaire feigns sickness and talks of
the waters of Plombieres, which would be of service
to him. Frederick replies that the springs of Glatz,
in Moravia, will be excellent for the re-establishment
of his health. A few days pass by. Voltaire, determined to escape the claws of royal friendship, again
sends his insignia to Frederick and chooses for his
leave-taking the very moment when Frederick was
reviewing his troops.

"Thus, you are determined to go?" abruptly said
the king. "Very well, then, sir, fare ye well."

Voltaire hastened away, and started in the direction
of Strasburg by way of Frankfort-on-the-Main.

The king of Prussia worried over Voltaire's de-
parture. He would have kept him at his court and
disciplined him as his soldiers; and, finding that
impossible, he contrived a very disagreeable surprise
for the departing philosopher.

Delighted with having regained his liberty, Voltaire was flying at high speed, when, to his great
stupefaction and lively indignation, he was on the
25th May, 1753, arrested as a malefactor, searched,
consigned to his hotel at Frankfort, and guarded
bodily by the resident of the king of Prussia, in the
name of the sovereign who accused him with nothing less than having defrauded him of his papers,
his poetical pieces, his literary masterpieces, and
even his state secrets.

Voltaire justified himself from these pretended thefts without difficulty. He gave up to the resident some letters of Frederick and a volume of poems given him by the king at Postdam, but he remained a prisoner in the *Lion d' Or* until the answer of the king had come.

His niece, Madame Denis, who waited for her uncle in Strasburg, having learned that he was a prisoner at Frankfort, hastened on to meet him.

Voltaire, in whom patience was not a chief virtue, became impatient with the tardiness, doubtless calculated, with which Frederick was answering his resident Freitag, and escaped from the *Golden Lion*. But Freitag overtook him and had him led back into a city building, where he was closely guarded together with his niece. Soldiers mounted guard around Madame Denis' bed. All the luxuriant arbitrariness of the Prussian agents is detailed in the letters of Voltaire on that occurrence. He mimics the *monsir* and the *poeshie* of the satellites of the king, describes their officious and swaggering brutality toward a woman, and depicts the nights of Madame Denis, who had sentinels for chambermaids and bayonets for bed-curtains, etc.

At last came the order of liberation from the king, and Voltaire was enabled to go on his way with Madam Denis. He escaped scot-free with the exception of the fright, and Frederick had the ridicule of having uselessly committed an act of arbitrariness.

Voltaire doubtless made the philosophical reflection that it is sometimes dangerous to become too familiar with kings who have two hundred thousand grenadiers at their service.

On his side the king consoled himself by saying of

the philosopher, "He is a man good to read, but dangerous to know. . . ."

Nevertheless Voltaire had done well to escape the despotism of the king of Sans-Souci, when he had felt it weighing too heavily upon him. Frederick was a great man in all the acceptation of the word. Admirable warrior, with the eye of an eagle, legislator, creator of a people, powerful mind, learned, lettered, Freethinker, turning his court into a refuge for proscribed philosophers, savants, and encyclopedists. But he had a rough and despotic hand, and often, also, a fantastic temper. That singular sovereign united all contrasts within himself, going from poetry to public business, from a philosophical discussion to a review, rhyming and writing memoirs in camp for his Berlin academy, a thundering Jove and pipe-playing Apollo, as austere as a Spartan, depraved and licentious at his private suppers, hiding his library behind a superb parade-bed, and sleeping upon a stretcher, dressing himself, and having hardly a single menial to wait upon him. He has in history neither a copy nor a parallel; not even in Julius Cæsar, who, like him, was au Epicurean and a Stoician by turns, a learned and shrewd man, a skilful general, with unheard-of muscular and mental activity, and, like him, absolute and a despot.

But Cæsar hastened the dissolution of the Roman empire, while Frederick founded a kingdom on the strong bases of science and free thought.

Indeed, it was with truth Madame du Chatelet had said that the king of Prussia was a phenomenon upon a throne; and Voltaire declared that there were two men in Frederick—Alexander and the abbé Cotin; Cæsar and Pradon.

After having received from the friendship of Frederick as painful a blow as that inflicted on him some years previous by Madame du Chatelet, Voltaire wandered from Plombières to Strasburg, then to Colmar, where the bishop excommunicated him.

On the 15th of November, 1754, he had an interview in Lyons with *his hero*, the Duke of Richelieu, whom he consulted and sounded upon the practicability of his return to Paris. But it is probable that the answer was a negative one, for Voltaire, immediately after the interview, made ready to leave France.

Unable to return to Paris, which was forbidden him by the Jesuitic faction, Voltaire once more resigned himself to exile.

Again he had to seek a refuge of liberty, a shelter against the intolerance of his countrymen, to whom he gave this last affectionate adieu, "I leave you, *arlequins anthropophages !*"

In Lyons, however, he had been gratified by numerous testimonies of sympathy, at which he must have felt satisfaction. He had been elected a member of the Academy of Sciences and Arts of that city. Besides, his *Merope* and his *Brutus* had been played at the great theater of Lyons, and as soon as the author had shown himself he had been greeted with acclamations. But having obtained positive proofs of the bitter hostility of the cardinal-archbishop of Zenia and of the governor of Lyons, he said to his secretary, "My friend, this country is not made for me."

This time our wandering philosopher found a retreat in Switzerland, where he simultaneously bought two estates—Monrion, near Lausanne, his winter quarters, and at the doors of Geneva, his summer residence, Mont-Saint-Jean, which he also called the *Delights*.

XIII.

As Antæus regained strength whenever he touched the earth, so did Voltaire regain all his vigor in the land of exile. His life in Switzerland, at the " Delights" and Monrion, was one of constant struggle and toil. He sent numerous articles to the Encyclopedia, with letters of encouragement to its brilliant corps of collaborators. Every day, the Encyclopedia was threatened in its existence. The Jesuitic party howled ceaselessly against its editors, and strove continually to raise against them the wrath of clergy, court, and parliament.

In the eyes of fanatics and of the ignorant multitude, the name of Encyclopedist was synonymous with son of Satan and highway robber. Voltaire exhorted his friends to union and cheerfulness in the struggle against the wretch (*l'infame*).

"Patience and courage," he wrote to D'Alembert and Diderot. "God will help us if we are united and cheerful. The *brethren* must dine together at least once a week."

Denis Diderot was the corner stone of that philosophical temple, of that new universal repertory of sciences, arts, and industry, of that Encyclopedia he had conceived while in the dungeon of Vincennes where he had been thrown in expiation of his *Letter on the Blind,* and which he brought to a successful issue after thirty years assiduous labor and struggles

with numberless obstacles and stormy persecutions.
Voltaire's letters breathe the most hearty sympathy and admiration for Diderot, that Vulcan
of intellectual labor, full of wit and gaiety, a
valiant worker, disinterested and modest, always
in the field, sharpening, hammering without ceasing
the philosophical steel, and meanwhile inaugurating
the Domestic Drama by producing *The Father of a
Family*, not allowing himself to become embittered
by bad fortune, as Rousseau did, but laughing in
its very face, giving his iron soul up to every noble
enthusiasm, and revolving, digesting all ideas in his
cyclopedic mind.   Between Voltaire and Diderot,
between these two companions in the same task,
there never rose the least cloud of misunderstanding
or distrust.

The intelligent burghers of Geneva soon became
assiduous frequenters of the *House of Delights*.
Some Parisians came there too, D'Alembert among
others, and the celebrated actor, LeKain, who
played the principal part in a new play of Voltaire's, *The Chinese Orphan*.   The lord of the
Mansion of Delights made friends by amusing and
treating everybody well.   "If Socrates," he was
wont to say, "had kept open house, his enemies,
far from putting him to death, would have invited
him to dinner."

His intellectual activity was prodigious.   Whilst
assiduously contributing to the Cyclopedia, he commenced the publication of his *Philosophical Dictionary*, and terminated his *Essay upon the Morals
and Intellect of Nations*, the pages of which are all
impressed with a vigorous hate for despotism,
fanaticism, and all that enslaves and deceives man.

In this masterpiece Voltaire created or rather re-suscitated history by rejecting the marvelous, the divine *sceneric*, the providential plan of Bossuet, as well as the palingenesiac and fatalistic systems. He showed in history a mixture of good and evil, madness and reason, progress and retrogression, the natural product of human liberty. One thing must be noted here—this important and original work had been commenced at Brussels at the request of Madame du Chatelet, who had been desirous of seeing the metamorphoses, the successive variations, the modifications and changes of morals, customs, laws and ideas, unfolding themselves in the pages of a truly philosophical book.

According to Voltaire, history in its essence is scarcely more than an extravagance, a madness with a method, a heap of crimes, of follies, and misfor-tunes, amongst which are witnessed some examples of virtue, some periods of happiness. Its panoramas show us error and prejudice lording it over truth and reason, the skilful and the strong reducing the weak to bondage and crushing the unfortunate, and the powerful themselves becoming in their turn the toys of fate as well as the slaves over which they rule. Finally, men becoming somewhat enlightened, and profiting by their experiences, their follies, errors, and misfortunes, learn to reflect. But the world walks like a turtle toward common sense and wis-dom. It advances and retreats alternately, and the same follies seem destined to reappear from time to time on the stage of history.

We have here a theory of history far more real and true than the supposititious order of straightfor-ward and uninterrupted progress, which has been the theme of so many modern historians, but which is refuted by retrogradations and deteriorations as frequent, radical, and natural in the life of societies as they are in the individual man.

"The history of kings and of battles has alone been chronicled," wrote Voltaire; "the history of nations has not been written. Do our laws, our customs, our intelligence count for nought?"

The *Essay on Morals* created lively sympathies for its author. At a later period the importance and success of this work was recalled when Voltaire's portrait was engraved on a medal of which the exergue bore these words, "HE TAKES AWAY FROM THE NATIONS THE BANDAGE OF ERROR."

All this while Voltaire's resentment of the Teutonic manner in which he had been treated at Frankfort by the king of Prussia had not diminished. Still under the same feeling of irritation he abused Frederick in several letters, giving him the name of *Duc* after an ape which he had in his mansion of the *Delights*. Besides, he wrote a pamphlet upon the freaks and secret vices of the king of Prussia, which pamphlet remained in his *Memoirs*, and was only published after his death.

Withal, Voltaire could not entirely forget the good hearty hours of effusion he had whiled away with the Solomon of the north, nor the close communion of their philosophic belief. Therefore he was much moved when he learned of the military disasters of Frederick, who, almost at the beginning of the Seven Years' War, at Kollin, the 18th of June, 1757, had been completely beaten and routed by the Austrians. He wrote to him. Frederic thanked him for the part he took in his misfortunes. Soon after, Voltaire received a letter from Wilhelmine, the Margravine of Bayreuth, informing him that the king, her father, despairing of triumph over his enemies, had resolved to kill himself. This was confirmed by Frederick's own hand, who said in a letter, half rhyme and half prose, according to his custom,

> " If I must to the wall,
>   The storm I will defy ;
> And, like a king, whate'er befall,
>   Will think, and live, and die."

And further:

> " I am a man. Enough ! for sorrow being born,
>   To fate I shall oppose my courage and my scorn."

"But, with all these sentiments, I am very far from condemning Cato and Otho. The last had but one beautiful moment — it was that of his death."

Voltaire energetically fought the dark resolution of Frederick by saying that suicide was a mean door through which to escape the difficulties of life. He gave him advice full of good sense, and did not spare him rugged truths.

"You would die ! And you love glory ! How can you think of an act which will deprive you of glory's crown ? I have already represented to you the sorrows of your friends, the triumphs of your enemies.

"I must add that nobody will look upon you as a martyr of liberty. We must be just toward ourselves. You know in how many courts they persist in looking at your entrance into Saxony as a trespass against the rights of nations. What will be said at these courts ?

"A man who is but a king might believe himself very unfortunate. But a philosopher can do without estates. Would it be worth while to be a philosopher if you could not bear adversity?"

Surrounded with victorious enemies, who had wrested Breslau from him; having on his shoulders Russia, Austria, Saxony, and France, the situation of the Prussian king was really critical, desperate, even, and he must have judged it so to have decided to write to the Marshal de Richelieu, who had been notified and prepared by Voltaire, the following letter:

"I know, sir duke, that you have not been put where you are in order to negotiate. I am, nevertheless, well persuaded that the nephew of the great Cardinal Richelieu is made to sign treaties just as well as to win battles. The matter is but a trifle—it is to make peace if it be so desired. I send you Mr. Delchetet, bearer of proposals, and in whom you can have full confidence. The man who has deserved statues at Genoa, who has conquered Minorca, can do nothing more glorious than to work for the restoration of peace to Europe. Be sure that nobody will be more thankful for it than your true friend,

"FREDERICK."

The king of Prussia was skilfully striving to detach France from the coalition formed against him. It would have been in the interests of France to negotiate at that very moment and withdraw from the Seven Years' War. But nothing was done. Frederick neither made peace nor killed himself. He only threw some verses—some flowers of rhetoric—over his still empty sarcophagus. Thanks to his military genius, he routed his enemies one after another, completely beat them all, and in a short time P. issia rose victorious out of a mighty struggle in whi h it had been near perishing, body and soul.

The refugee of *Monrion* and the Deligh s was still spoken of in Paris. His successive works exploded like shells in the midst of the gay city. Vainly did he deny their paternity, his style, his mann r, his fearful and destructive raillery, were too easily recognized to allow of a mistake. The *Pucelle* made a terrible noise. From his residence of the Delights Voltaire protested, while he secretly directed the destruction of the manuscript, which was done by a friend. But his translation into verses of the Canticles from the book of Ecclesiastes, which he had signed, was declared licentious and an insult to the Bible and to religion. The Parliament of Paris condemned the book to the fagot. All the Jesuits and clerical pamphleteers, Nonotte, Berthier, Fréron, Pompignan, Terray, Chaumaix, Vernet, La Baumelle, Patouillet, Larcher, Sabatier, Ribalier, Cogé, the whole Roman Catholic band, fell unbridled upon Voltaire.

He became the target of the obscurantints, of the hirelings of the church. They preserved or at least affected a certain forbearance for other Freethinkers, but they kept up a fire upon the general, upon him who incessantly repeated to his co-laborers, "*Ecrasons l'infame*" (*Let us crush the wretch*). But what superb replies, what terrific retorts ! Woe to those who dared to attack Voltaire. He transfixed his enemies with his feathered arrows, he nailed them to the pillory of their own infamy. Scarcely had he received and read their pamphlets when the mail of Geneva carried toward Paris the scathing, the stunning replies which made the whole population of Paris laugh at the expense of the Jesuitic writers. "My God, render our enemies very ridiculous!" was the habitual prayer of Voltaire. But as Providence was somewhat derelict and given to being slow, he helped her by throwing ridicule upon his adversaries, poisoning them with their own venom, and transfixing them with his keen epigrams.

The *auto-da-fe* of Voltaire's works took place at Geneva as well as in Paris. Upon the energetic remonstrances of the consistory, the Great Council caused *Candide* and the *Pucelle* to be thrown to the fire. The rigorist party, conducted by evangelical ministers, remonstrated against the presence of Voltaire upon Swiss territory and attributed to him a corrupting influence. The friends of Voltaire in Geneva were called *relaxed*. A commission was appointed to decide upon the necessity and urgency of expelling him from the canton.

Voltaire began to conceive a keen hatred against that fanatic and demented republic, which he called the dwarf, the fetus of republics.

Being never caught napping, and (very happily for him, for otherwise he would have experienced the same fate as his writings) abounding in expedients, Voltaire contrived to elude and disconcert the *rigorists* of the evangelical consistory by buying two properties in France, one at Tournay, the other at Ferney, at one hour's distance from the Swiss frontier. Thenceforward he had his quadrilateral, his strategical position.

"My left wing rests on Mount Jura," he writes to D'Alembert, "my right on the Alps, and I have the Geneva lake in front of my camp, a good castle on the border of France, the Delights on the Genevese soil, and a good house in Lausanne. Creeping thus from one resort to the other I foil the kings, . . . for," added he, " philosophers should always have two or three holes under ground to shelter them from the hounds."

Indeed, for such a thrifty and adventurous philosopher as Voltaire it was good to be astride of two frontiers. When Calvinistic intolerance threatened him in Switzerland, he took refuge on the French border, at Ferney. Was it, on the contrary, the wind of Catholic intolerance that blew with fury, he passed over into Switzerland.

Voltaire always strove to escape his enemies, the *harlequins anthropophages*, and he invariably succeeded.

As if Voltaire had not already adversaries enough, Jean Jacques Rousseau at last took part with them. During twelve years the intercourse of the two philosophers had been amicable. Diderot, the Prometheus, creator of men, had launched Jean Jacques in the arena, and Voltaire, who during his whole life sustained with all his strength the champions of thought, had cordially encouraged him, having never gone beyond meekly railing at the author of the *Discourse on Arts and Sciences* by writing to him that his publications made him feel like walking on all fours.

Voltaire had many times, but unsuccessfully, invited Rousseau to come and rest himself in his hermitage and *to breathe the pure air* of the Delights.

Rousseau committed the great wrong of joining the clerical pack- against Voltaire and the Cyclopedists. It was, so to speak, forordained that Voltaire should find all the Rousseaus in his way. Jean Jacques accused him of having corrupted Geneva, his birth-place, in exchange for the hospitality he had received there; just as Jean Baptiste Rousseau had formerly attributed the intention of spreading Atheism in the Netherlands, to the man who had said, " If God did not exist, it would be necessary to invent him." Taking his text from a poem written by Voltaire upon the earthquake of Lisbon, Mcquinez, and Tetuan, which, in 1755, had made so many thousand victims, the high priest Jean-Jacques had said the work was an insult to Providence and an attack against the deity, and that simply because the author of the *Disaster of Lisbon* had affirmed that everything was not for the best in the best of possible worlds, and that our globe was afflicted with physical and moral wrong !

Ah! most unhappy men, O thou unhappy earth,
Of all the plagues most sad, most frightful, ghostly hearth;
Of aimless pangs and wounds, O thou drear, ceaseless knell;
False sages who persist in crying, all is well!

But war was really kindled between the two champions by an article in the *Cyclopedie* emanating from the pen of D'Alembert, who recommended to the Genevans the foundation of a theater and dramatic performances as a means of culture and polish.

Immediately Jean Jacques published his famous *Letter on dramatic performances*, which according to that dramatic author were the perdition, and caused the demoralization of, human kind.

Such a paradox was sharply refuted by Voltaire, just as he had already riddled through and through the absurd theories brought forward by Jean Jacques, who would have had humanity retrograde to its very cradle.

In fact, the first work of Rousseau, apart from his grandiloquent style, ought to have been signed by Freron or by the Jesuit Nonotte. He had condemned civilization and held the primitive state of man up to our admiration by trying to prove the sciences and arts to hav been a source of corruption and social decadence.

Nevertheless, it was readily understood that Rousseau had only reviled civilization to render his criticism of society more stinging, and, in consequence, · the philosophical group did not entertain any ill will toward him.

Under pretense of exonerating himself from having authorized the printing of his strictures upon the *Disaster of Lisbon*, Rousseau wrote to Voltaire a letter which ended with a declaration of hatred against him, as well as stinging reproaches for having perverted and alienated his (Rousseau's) native land! The foolish missive ended as follows: "I do not like you, sir; you have wronged me in every way and have goaded me wherever I, your disciple and your enthusiastic admirer, was most sensitive. You have ruined Geneva as a return for the asylum it had given you; you have alienated from me my fellow-citizens as a reward for the praises which I had prodigally bestowed upon you in their very midst.

"You alone it is who have rendered life in my own country unbearable to me; you will cause me to die in a foreign land, deprived of all the consolations of dying men, and my body will be thrown into the common grave as the sole honor it deserves, while you will, in my very native land, enjoy all the honors that a man may expect."

It is easy to see by the tenor of this letter that Jean Jacques was jealous of the fame and of the friends Voltaire had won in Switzerland.

"Our friend Jean Jacques is in poorer health than I thought," replied Voltaire. "He needs neither advisers nor attendants, but baths and broths."

And on the 22d of April, 1761, he wrote from Ferney to Mr. Damilaville: "I am an admirer of Mr. Diderot, because to his profound knowledge he adds the merit of not affecting the philosopher, and because he has always been enough of a philosopher not to bow down to the infamous prejudices which disgrace human reason. But when a Jean Jacques, a very Diogenes, emerges from the depths of his slime to declaim against comedy, after having written comedies himself (and detestable ones at that); when this waggish fellow has the insolence of of writing me that I am corrupting the morals of his country; when he gives himself airs of loving his country (which does not care a fig for him); and when finally this wretch, after three times having changed religion, concocts with some Socinian priests of the city of Geneva to prevent the few Genevese who have any talent to come and exercise it in my house (which is *not* in his little territory of Geneva), he transgresses all bounds and gives us the sight of the most despicable fool I have ever known.

"This is, dear sir, what I openly think, and what I beg you to say to Mr. Diderot."

In the polemical arena Voltaire knew no restraint. He became exceedingly embittered against Jean Jacques, calling him a fool and a false brother, publishing against him *The Geneva War* and other writings, taxing him with immorality, which was not true, and reproaching him with having abandoned the two children he had from Therese Levasseur, which was true.

In his *Letters on the Mountain*, Rousseau complains against the Geneva government, taxing it with tolerating the *dangerous writings* of Voltaire while prosecuting his.

"It is not I who have desired war," writes Voltaire; "I would never have begun it." And in another letter: "How we would have cherished that fool had he not been a false brother!"

When the fire of their animosity somewhat passed away the two philosophers appreciated each other better.

"It is not that he lacks genius," said Voltaire of Jean Jacques, "but it is genius allied to evil genius."

"His first movements are good," said Rousseau in his turn; "it is only by reflection that he grows wicked."

Voltaire had a temper of incredible vivacity, and in polemics he was pitiless and cruel; but soon got over his fits of passion. After one of these acts of vivacity with a friend, he said to him: "Forgive me. I am more to be pitied than you. It is not blood that runs in my veins; it is vitrol."

As soon as Jean Jacques was threatened in his liberty by the publication of his *Emile*, Voltaire offered him a refuge in Ferney. Rousseau harshly repulsed the fraternal hand stretched out to him.

"He outrages me at pleasure," wrote Voltaire to a friend. "I had offered him not an asylum, but a house in which he could have lived as my brother."

Although Voltaire pushed his animosity too far, the first blame in this quarrel must fall upon Jean

Jacques Rousseau. His misanthropy and surly temper, although well explained and extenuated by the misfortunes of his life, were the factors which led him sometimes to join the chorus of Voltaire's enemies.

Jean Jacques was a suffering soul, a dark dreamer, speculative, subjective, sentimental, lachrymatory, connecting everything with his personality, believing that the whole of mankind had conspired for his ruin. His sickly imagination, his excessive sensibility, his bashfulness and backwardness, greatly increased the real misfortunes of his existence, which was but a painful poem from beginning to end. This philosopher who too often wallowed in the rut of vice while he possessed the enthusiasm of virtue; this reformer who three times changed his form of worship, and still kept a measure of religion; this apologist of maternity and childhood, who adored other people's children but abandoned his own; this artisan's boy, this lacquey* with an unbending pride, breaks off with all his friends, even with Diderot, who had not the time to quarrel with any one; this philosopher who began his career like a Lefranc de Pompignan, by attacking Voltaire and the philosophers, presents a mass of contradictions and as many inconsistencies as a harlequin's dress. He is especially in a state of antagonism with his times, satirical, skeptical, and jocular as they were. Yet he opened for them well-springs of sentiment and magnificent vistas, which, although only made up of the substance of his dreams and illusions, brought

---

*Rousseau, during his stay in Italy, had been for some time attached as a servant to the Countess of Vercelli.

his dandified generation back to the truth and simplicity of nature, which conventional trappings disguised or altogether hid.

The genius and misfortunes of Rousseau have gone far to cancel his faults. His life was a succession of undeserved persecutions and humiliations, of miseries and blamable deeds, just as his works are compounds of paradoxes, sophisms, and eloquent truths. At the moment when he appears, Voltaire's powerful sarcasm having battered down a great many strongholds of iniquity and error, the new comer attempts the reconstruction of the ideal city. In his *Contrat Social* he lays the foundation of the edifice, the corner-stone of the sovereignty of the people. In his *Emile* he shows that the reform of education is the necessary preface, the inevitable antecedent of the democracy. In his *Nouvelle Heloise* he moves and bring tears to the eyes of women, who become his impassioned readers.

His ideas were for the most part drawn from Locke's philosophical books, as Mr. Villemain has so justly remarked. But he has developed them with the passionate eloquence and the contagious pathos that were the stamp of his admirable genius.

Although Rousseau's influence cannot be compared with Voltaire's—for it must not be forgotten that Voltaire, workman of the first hour, had made the breach through which Rousseau could pass—posterity has settled the quarrel of the two great philosophers by comprehending them in one and the same admiration.

Jean Jacques died in July, 1778, six weeks after Voltaire. The National Assembly in 1791 united their remains in the Pantheon, and the Catholic reaction threw their ashes to the same breeze.

Their immediate posterity had cast a shadow over a man who during his whole lifetime had been pleased to forget himself—the great, the immortal Diderot, resuscitated later in Danton. Now only is the star of the creator of the *Encyclopedie* rising on the horizon of fame, and it is but justice that it should at last shine brilliantly in the intellectual firmament.

Diderot is modern, *actuel*, as well as Voltaire, while Rousseau has largely grown old on account of his arbitrary idealism, his religious sentimentalism, and his mysticism. His *Utopia* has had its day as well as that of Thomas More. He started from a false *a priori*, from an entity, an abstraction of impossible realization—the primitive state of man. Contrary to Saint-Simon, who saw progress and the terrestrial paradise before us in the future, Jean Jacques placed his ideal in I do not know what Spartan republic and Beotian state. Upon this he erected chimerical structures which cannot stand examination.

Voltaire did not search after either an ideal land or an ideal society. The question for him was, before anything else, *to cultivate his garden*, as Candide used to say; to rid it from the Catholic brambles, from the tares of old customs and old prejudices; to give to this new soil sun, air, light, and mold, and to rid all the moral fruit trees from caterpillars and other kinds of parasitic insects.

"Destroy, destroy all you can," he wrote to D'Alembert. "In so doing you will serve at once the state and philosophy."

In fact it was necessary to throw down the tottering hovels, to clear the social soil from its old oppressions and superannuated systems. Voltaire and Diderot did not pretend to found the new society on any precise basis beyond that of science, liberty, and justice, leaving to the future generations a free field for reconstruction and reorganization. "Everything through liberty!" was their motto, and it was a good one. If in this Herculean duty, as Auguste Comte has said, Diderot was the Atlas who bore the eighteenth century on his broad shoulders, Voltaire was the head of the giant, the shrewd, dissecting mind; and from the year 1718 to 1778, during sixty years, he ceased not to struggle a single day, a single hour.

Voltaire and Diderot were not only philosophers and literary men, but also *men of action*, who were molding their time and preparing the future. These soldiers of the mind had a love of battle; they threw themselves briskly and joyfully into the conflict of the day. Jean Jacques offers a perfect contrast to them. He keeps aloof from the army, he remains away from the Encyclopedic battalion, and fights by himself. Metaphysician, exclusive ideologist that he is, he hates to struggle, and when compelled to face the enemy he does it only with groans and melancholy complaints upon his sad destiny. He plows his solitary furrow apart from and outside of contemporary events. He applies himself to the study of primitive propensities, human passions, and politi-al theories. The last he stamped with religion, mixing and confounding the two, making one the antecedent and mistress of the other, whereas Voltaire and Diderot completely rejected the alliance of religion and politics, endeavoring to free the political

and social elements from all worships, from all theo-
logical bondage.   It is in this way that the hermit
and the dreamer, the metaphysician Jean Jacques,
grubbed up a forsaken corner of the philosophical
field of the eighteenth century.

We do not forget that Rousseau, with all his utopian dreams and his religio-political fancies, did
his share of the great work of his century by giving
the death-blow to the worship of personal power, by
putting the axe to the royal and seignorial tree, and
to social privileges especially, by making of education
the peristyle of the new society.   Nature, aided by
the misfortunes he underwent in the course of his
painful existence, trained him so as to make of him
a representative of the people and the living and
speaking expression of the democracy.

These three—Voltaire, Diderot, and Rousseau—
supported by the phalanx of the Encyclopedists, were
according to their different temperaments, the archi-
tects of a radical revolution of the human mind.

XIV.

Voltaire resided in turns now on the French frontier, now in the country of Gex, or at the Delights. In Tournay he gave free vent to his taste for the theater, and organized dramatic performances. Notwithstanding Rousseau's denunciations, a great number of Genevans took part as performers in his troupe.

, Bringing out comedies did not cause Voltaire to forget his philosophical aims, and he pursued them with ardor by ceaselessly stimulating the zeal of all Freethinkers. He wrote to D'Alembert in 1757:

"I do as Cato did of old. I always end my harangue by saying, *Deleatur Carthago*. It wants only five or six well united philosophers to throw down the colossus. The question is not to prevent our servants going to mass or to sermon; it is to free the heads of families from the tyranny of impostors and to diffuse the spirit of toleration. This great cause has already met with inspiring success. The vineyard of truth is well cultivated by the D'Alemberts, the Diderots, the Bolingbrokes, the Humes, etc. If the king of Prussia had been willing to confine himself to that holy work he would have lived happy, and all the academicians of Europe would have blessed him."

And later he wrote to the same:

"I hav suffered for forty years the outrages of the bigots and blackguards. I have seen there is nothing to be won by moderation ; it is folly to think it.

We must make war and, if need be, die like men and
fall upon the heap of the bigots we have slain."

At that time Frederick wrote from Siberia the letter in which he expresses such a true appreciation of
the sympathetic genius of Voltaire:

"Shall I speak you soft? I will tell you the
truth. I see in you the most beautiful genius the
ages have produced. I admire your verses. I
like your prose; above all, those little detached
pieces in your *Miscellanies of Literature*. Never
before had an author so fine a tact or a taste as correct and as delicate as yours. You are charming in
conversation; you know how to interest and amuse at
the same time. You are the most seductive creature
I know, able to make yourself loved by everybody, if you choose. There is so much gracefulness
in your wit that you can offend and at the same time
gain the indulgence of those who know you.
Finally, you would be perfect if you were not a
man."

Another cloud passed over the renewed friendship
of the two philosophers, as we learn from a sentence
in a letter from Voltaire to Theriot, July 7, 1760:

"The Solomon of the North always loves to write
in prose or verse, and in whatever situation he may
find himself; but I could not bring him to atone, by
the slightest gallantry, for the unworthy treatment
inflicted upon my niece in Frankfort."

To that complaint of Voltaire Frederick had rudely
replied:

"If you had not had to deal with a fool in love
with your beautiful genius, you would not have gotten so well out of the matter with any one else.
A word to the wise is sufficient, and now let me hear

no more of that niece who worries me and who has not as much merit as her uncle to cover up her faults."

This calling up of the irritating past brought a stop in the correspondence between Voltaire and Frederick. The king of Prussia would never own that he had been in the wrong in the Frankfort affair.

Voltaire installed himself at Ferney, where he was to reside for such a long time, in September, 1760. He inaugurated his patriarchate of Ferney by a generous action. Having learned that a granddaughter of the great Corneille was in very poor circumstances, he took her to his house, educated her, became her school-master, and lastly married her to a rich gentleman of the country of Gex. It turned out that Marie Corneille was not the granddaughter, but only a collateral relative of the great tragical poet of the seventeenth century. One degree more or less in consanguinity could be but of little importance to Voltaire when good was to be accomplished.

Nothing is more touching than his correspondence about his adopted daughter. Let us give some extracts. To Mr. Lebrun, who, in an ode, had asked him to take care of the granddaughter of the great Corneille, he wrote:

"I shall limit myself to tell you in prose how I like your ode and your proposition. It is only fitting for an old follower of Corneille to try to be useful to the granddaughter of his general."

To the Count of Argental:

"We are very well satisfied with *Miss Rodogune.* We find her natural, lively, and true. Her nose resembles that of Mme. de Ruffec. She has also the same roguish face, but more beautiful eyes, a nicer skin, to which add a large mouth, tolerably appetizing, with two ranks of faultless pearls. If somebody has the pleasure to approach these teeth with his I wish it to be rather a Catholic than a Huguenot."

Later, to the same:

"My arms are loaded down with troublesome affairs, and my most difficult business is to teach grammar to Miss Corneille, who has no disposition at all for that sublime science."

Still to the same:

"The philosopher who intends to marry *us* (he speaks of the first pretender to the hand of Marie Corneille) will arrive to-morrow. We will prim up Miss Cornelie Chiffon; we will adorn her. She pretends she will know a little orthography; it is already something for a philosopher. Well, we will do the best we can ; adventures of that kind always settle themselves. There is a providence for girls."

To Mr. de Mairan:

"That young person has as much artlessness as Pierre Corneille had of the grand air. Some one was reading *Cinna* to her the other day, when she heard this verse, 'I love you, Emily, and may heaven crush me . . .' 'Fie !' said she, 'do not pronounce those ugly words.' 'It is from your uncle,' they answered her.' So much the worse,' said she; 'is it thus one speaks to his affianced ?'"

To d'Argenteuil:

" . . . Let me revive my spirits; I am exhausted. I have just come from a ball. I am not master of my senses.—A ball, old fool, a ball in thy mountains ! And to whom hast thou given it ? to the badgers ?—No, if you please, to a very good company.

Le droit du Seigneur (the lord's right) has delighted three hundred persons of all ages and conditions, lords, farmers, bigots, and gallant women. They came from Lyons, Dijon, and Turin. Would you believe that Miss Corneille carried all the suffrages? How natural, lively, joyful she was! How she mastered her audience, striking the ground with her foot when not readily prompted. I acted the bailiff, and, may it not displease you, did it so as to make them split with laughter. . . ."

To Damilaville:

"We marry Miss Corneille to a gentleman of the neighborhood, an officer of dragoons, possessing 10,-000 livres of income, or about that, in landed property at Ciderville, at the door of Ferney. I will harbor them both. We are all happy. I am ending my life like a true patriarch."

Voltaire had other adopted children besides Marie Corneille; we mean the valiant phalanx of the Encyclopedists who were struggling in Paris against wind and tide. From Ferney, Voltaire sustained them, sent them articles, took part in their struggle. His letters made an ardent propaganda and were all terminated by the watchword, " *Ecr. l'inf.*" (*Let us crush the wretch*), with his habitual abbreviation.

"Above all, *crush the wretch*," he writes D'Alembert at the end of a correspondence. "And remember well that if you do not crush him, he will crush you."

But *the infamous* was not easily crushed. The heads of the hydra were always renewing themselves, and menaced the champions of science and Freethought. The archbishop of Paris had fulminated an outrageous circular against the Encyclopedists and

all their co-laborers, who were threatened with banishment. Had it not been for the influence of the
duke of Choiseul, the Encyclopedia, which, indeed,
had already been suspended, would have been suppressed. Morellet and Marmontel had been thrown
into the Bastille. Helvetius' book, *The Mind*, had
been burned by the hand of the executioner. Rousseau's *Emile* had met with the same fate. Furthermore, its author had been condemned to arrest by the
Parliament of Paris "for having subjected religion
to the examination of reason, and tried to destroy
the certainty of the miracles recorded in the holy
books, and also the infallibility and authority of
the church." Members of that persecuting Parliament had said, "Nothing will have been done as long
as the authors are not burnt together with their
books."

Rousseau, having escaped from France, intended
to take refuge in Geneva, his birthplace. But he
was literally caught between two fires; for a short
time after the decree of the French Parliament,
rendered in 1762, the great Council of Geneva, without even having read his *Emile*, caused it to be burnt,
as it had been in Paris. It was then that Rousseau,
paraphrasing the words of Brutus, could have exclaimed, "O Republic, thou art but a name—an
empty word!"

After wandering among the mountains of Switzerland in quest of a shelter, Rousseau found an asylum
in the canton of Neufchatel by placing himself under
the protection of the king of Prussia. He soon left
Switzerland, however, to go to England and reside
with Hume, with whom, unhappily, he did not remain long on friendly terms.

Voltaire had projected to draw the Encyclopedists away from the tormented life of Paris and the dangers that threatened them every day by founding at Cleves a republic of philosophers, destined to become a new Sunium—a second Salenta. The king of Prussia had given his assent to the scheme.

D'Alembert, frightened or wearied out, had retired from the Encyclopedia. The indefatigable Diderot had remained alone at the head of a small company of obscure co-laborers, who very carefully hid their names and their participation in that dictionary of sciences and arts, exposed, as it was, to the thunder-bolts of Parliament and clergy.

Voltaire wrote to Damilaville: "I do not doubt that if you came and settled at Cleves with Plato (Diderot) and other friends, they would propose very advantageous conditions to you. They would put up a press capable of bringing out a great deal of work. They would establish another much more important manufacture—that of truth. Plato could go with his wife or his daughter, or leave them in Paris, at his option."

And to Diderot: "By going to Cleves you would exchange slavery for liberty. A man like you should regard only with horror the country in which it is your misfortune to live. Thinking and sensible beings ought to live in a corner of the world, sheltered from the absurd knaves who disfigure it."

To take Diderot away from his charming and intelligent wife, from his Café Procope, from his beloved Paris, from his philosophical workshop, was an impossible undertaking. So he replied to Voltaire that it was necessary to stay in Paris, fight the Roman Catholic monster face to face, on his own

ground, in spite of storms and perils; and the beautiful plan of a philosophical colony was abandoned.

———

XV.

Voltaire lived sixteen years in Ferney, and the
reader will appreciate what frightful ravages, what
moral disorders, these terrible Freethinkers occasioned wherever they set up their tent, when he
knows how Voltaire made of the miserable borough
of Ferney a very prosperous little town by building
three schools, patronizing agriculture and industry,
spreading case and comfort, and placing capital as
suggested to him by his large experience, profound
knowledge of things, and acute intellect.

His tenants, his numerous employes, as well as all
the land tillers surrounding Ferney, to whatever religion they belonged, Catholic or Protestant, loved
Voltaire. They consulted him concerning their private affairs. Whenever he went on his rounds
through the country he found himself surrounded by
them as by a family.

The country of Gex experiencing a famine after
an entirely sterile and unproductive season, Voltaire
distributed all the grain in his possession. He never
learned of a misfortune without hastening to alleviate
it. He was good, affable, humane with all. At
every turn he would loan money without the slightest
hope of being reimbursed. When unemployed
workmen knocked at his door he gave them work.
Numerous artisans having emigrated after the
grievous troubles of 1770, they found in the manor

at Ferney both refuge and employment. Voltaire had erected in the village several stocking and watch factories. Not content with being simply an agriculturist and horticulturist, he must also become a manufacturer.

Those who have accused Voltaire of coldness of heart, of false and ridiculous pride, do not know him or have refused to study his patriarchal life in Ferney.

To all the compliments that were paid him he was pleased to answer, "I have done a little good; it is my best work."

Justly proud of what he had accomplished, in 1761 he wrote to D'Alembert: "Yes, *Mordieu*, I serve God, for I love my country, for I erect schools, for I mean to erect an hospital, for *there are no longer any paupers* on my land, despite the revenue hounds."

The bishop of Annecy, who had the borough of Ferney in his diocese, was consumed with rage at the sight of a popular philosopher in the country of Gex, spreading around him happiness and well-being. He watched an opportunity which would allow him to bring down upon Voltaire the thunders of the church. That much desired occasion was not long in presenting itself.

Voltaire had always possessed architectural notions. He had formerly reconstructed Circy, for the present he was building and rebuilding Ferney. According to his plans, the old church, which masked the mansion, had to disappear. He caused another to be built, located it by the side of the theater, finding the parallel to his taste, and dedicated it to God with this inscription, "*Deo erexit Voltaire.*"

"The church I have had built," he said to the

Englishman, Richard Twis, "is the only church in the universe dedicated to God alone. All others are dedicated to the saints. For my part, I would rather build a church to the master than to the servants."

About a crucifix which he had painted anew, he wrote to Madame de Fontaine: "I am very sorry not to have you marry in my church in the presence of a large Jesus in gilt, with the mien of a Roman emperor, whose former silly expression of countenance I have taken away."

It was pretended he had given his own features to it, so that the good people who thought they were kneeling to Jesus did in reality worship Voltaire.

From time to time he took the fancy of catechising the peasants and peasant women of the neighborhood who came to his church. He preached sermons to them, inspiring them with horror for theft, then very common in the country of Gex; he also preached to them charity and toleration.

The officiating priest was sometimes the curate of Ferney, and sometimes Father Adam, a Jesuit to whom he had given the hospitality of his mansion. This man said mass, supervised the works, and played chess with Voltaire, who thrashed him whenever he was the loser.

The patriarch of Ferney had his two *beasts* in his mansion—the Abbé Voisenon, and the reverend Father Adam, who, said he, was not *the first man in the world.*

The bishop of Annecy brought against Voltaire the accusation of sacrilege for having erected a temple without canonical authorization—for having profaned the rites and ceremonies of religion by his unauthorized preaching. The clergy came to take away the holy sacrament, which, they said, had been desecrated. Furthermore, some women testified that in the presence of a cross from the old church Voltaire had exclaimed, "Take away that gibbet!" The sacrilege was denounced before the authorities at Gex, and the law made a descent upon the château of Ferney.

"I have hidden from you a part of my troubles," wrote Voltaire to the count of Argental, "but at last you must be aware that I have war with the clergy. I am building a tolerably good church, I founded a school, and, as a reward for my good deeds, a curate from a neighboring village, calling himself a *promoter*, and another curate who calls himself an *official*, have begun a criminal suit against me for one foot and a half of ground in a cemetery, and for two mutton chops which were mistaken for unearthed human bones.

"They wanted to excommunicate me for having moved a wooden cross from its place and insolently pulled down part of a barn which they pompously styled a parish church.

"As I love passionately to be master of the situation, I threw down the whole church in answer to the complaint of having pulled down half, then took away the bells, the altar, the confessionals, the baptistery, and sent my parishioners to go and hear mass three miles away.

"The prosecuting attorney and the procurator of the king came to me with a complaint. I sent them all to China. I made them understand they were egregious donkeys, as indeed they are. I had so taken my measures that the general procurator to the Parliament corroborated my assertions before them.

I am now about to have the honor of appealing against these abuses. . . . I believe I shall kill my bishop with grief, if he does not first die from superfluous fat. . . .

"You will note, if you please, that at the same time I apply to the pope for redress. My destiny is to baffle Rome and to make her subservient to my gracious will. The *Mahomet* affair encourages me.

"If my request to the pope and my letter to the Cardinal Passionei are ready when the mail leaves, I shall put them under my angel wings, who will have the kindness to forward my package to the duke of Choiseul, for I want him to laugh at these things and to stand by me. This negotiation will be easier to bring about honorably than peace."

Meanwhile the trial was preparing; the proceedings were sent by the bailiff to the Parliament of Dijon. But the intervention of influential persons fortunately prevented its continuance.

The bishop of Annecy had transmitted his complaint of sacrilege to the archbishop of Paris, who on that account asked, at Versailles, the expulsion of the philosopher of Ferney. The devout Maria Lesezinzka, at the instigation of the archbishop, urged Louis XV. to avenge the church by proscribing Voltaire. Louis XV., out of patience at last, replied to the fanatical queen:

"What would you have me do, Madame? If Voltaire were in Paris, I should banish him to Ferney."

Louis XV., desired but one thing, to be rid of Voltaire's presence.

The bishop of Annecy and his curates excited every day by their violent harangues the fanaticism of the credulous population against the *sacrilegious* patriot of Ferney. Voltaire took fright. He sought refuge in Switzerland. But he soon returned to Ferney with the resolution of foiling the bishop and his acolytes by a trick of his own. He put himself to bed, while his servants reported in the neighborhood that he he was very sick. Shortly after, he ordered a monk of the capuchins to be called in order to receive his confession; he also sent after a notary. The capuchin asked a permit from the bishop, who had forbidden either communion or absolution to be given to Voltaire.

But delighted with the prospect of soon being rid of such an adversary by death, the bishop raised the ban.

When the Capuchin entered Voltaire's room he trembled like a leaf. It seemed to him as if he had the devil himself to confess. "You will have to prompt me in my *credo* and my *confiteor*, which I have somewhat forgotten," said to him the dying man. The capuchin mumbled his Latin, and Voltaire repeated after him, after which he made his confession, which was nothing else than his own eulogy and glorification. He declared that during his whole life he had done nothing but good, and ordered the capuchin to give him the absolution, which was done. The curate of Ferney entering thereupon, the dying man received the extreme unction. Then he made the following declaration:

"Having my God in my mouth, I declare that I sincerely forgive all who have calumniated me to the king (this was meant for the bishop of Annecy), and have not succeeded in their bad designs, and I ask for a written affidavit from Raffo, notary public."

The ceremonial being at an end, every one left, well edified.

"Scarcely had everybody gone out of the castle, when," relates the secretary, Wagnière, "Mons. de Voltaire, with whom I had been left alone, said to me, as he nimbly jumped out of bed: 'I had some trouble with that scapegrace of a capuchin. But, after all, it was amusing, and can only do good. Let us take a walk through the garden.'"

Voltaire was not unused to this comedy of death. He had played it at Colmar, when excommunicated by the bishop of that city. Looking upon the ceremonies of Catholic worship as purely theatrical mummeries, and upon the priests as astute comedians, he felt no scruple in using their repertory and indulging in pasquinades to which he attached no real importance. His confession and receiving of the extreme unction at Ferney were thus a skilful retort at once to the accusation of sacrilege made by the bishop of Annecy, to the proceedings already had against him, and to the fanatical denunciations of the clergy.

Voltaire carried this irreligious jest as far as to have himself received as a capuchin and to send the benediction of the father capuchin of the country of Gex to several of his friends.

If, perchance, some severe censor feel tempted to condemn these comedies of Voltaire, let him not forget that these were at the worst only small spots on the resplendent sun, and served, besides, to shield him and help in some degree the accomplishment of his work.

Voltaire made no distinction between the several cohorts of the clerical band. In his eyes they possessed the same tendencies, the same vices, and the same final aims. However, he has observed that the Jesuits were conspicuous for their pride. Thus they oecame indignant and entirely lost their self-control if they heard themselves called *monks*. They did not wish to be confounded with the other monastic orders. In nearly all the philosopher's works the Jesuits are the butt of his keenest jests—of his most cutting raillery. In Ferney they pitted themselves against him. In the country of Gex, as elsewhere, the reverend fathers were given to inveigling and usurpation. They found Voltaire in their way. In 1761 their arch enemy wrote to the Marquis d'Argence: " I, indeed, have had the gratification of driving the Jesuits from a hundred acres of land out of which they had swindled the king's officers, but I cannot strip them of some lands they possessed previously, and which they obtained through the confiscation of a nobleman's property. Impossible to sever, at once, all the heads of the hydra !"

— —

XVI.

Voltaire exercised a veritable public ministry in Ferney. The numerous victims of fanaticism and judiciary errors having implored his intervention, he devoted himself to the redress of their wrongs. The patriarch of Ferney was not simply a thinker, a theorizer, but also a man of action, a knight cased in steel and fighting for the right. He stood always ready to throw himself into the thickest of the fight to redress the iniquities of his time.

At that period the Catholic party, wishing to strike the reformation to the heart and to extirpate it from the kingdom, had imagined nothing better than to accuse with imaginary crimes the Protestants, who, since the revocation of the edict of Nantes, were in a most precarious situation, being simply tolerated. Thus the parliaments cringingly subserved the wishes of the clergy and listened to the most iniquitous and false accusations.

First, it was the Protestant Calas (1761), condemned to the wheel by the Parliament of Toulouse, under the false accusation of having murdered his son, who, according to the denunciators, had been hung by his father for having avowed his purpose to apostatize and embrace the Catholic religion. Calas had been executed in Toulouse on the 9th of March, 1762.

After him came the turn of the Calvinist Sirven, from Castres, sentenced to death by the tribunal of Mazamet for having drowned his daughter, whom the Catholics had vainly tried to convert by martyrizing her in a convent, and who, in a fit of insanity resulting from her hardships, had accidentally thrown herself in a well.

Then the young De la Barre, son of an officer, and D'Etallonde, son of a presiding judge, were sentenced, in 1766, to the torture of the wheel for having insulted and damaged a wooden crucifix at one end of the bridge of Abbeville, in Picardy. D'Etallonde had escaped death by flight. De la Barre, after having had his tongue torn out, was decapitated and his body was thrown to the fagots, together with a copy of the *Philosophical Dictionary* of Voltaire. In the accusations, the latter had been denounced as the inspirer of the sacrilege.

All these judiciary crimes were at the same time the work of the Catholic party, of the Parliaments, and of detestable laws and judicial forms against which Voltaire had long and unceasingly protested by asking the revision of the criminal code.

The sage of Ferney took in hands the cause of the innocents stricken down by the parliaments and undertook their rehabilitation. He first published for this purpose his celebrated *Treatise on Tolerance, on the occasion of the death of Calas.*

More fortunate than Calas, Sirven and his family succeeded in escaping their persecutions. But at what price was this! What a painful odyssey, that of the Sirven family, the father fleeing in one direction, the wife and the daughter in another, the former being as long as three months before he could reach Geneva, and the latter being able to cross the Swiss frontiers after five months of hiding and fearful anxieties, under the very eye of fanaticism, watching and searching for them to deliver them up to the executioner. Where is a pen eloquent enough to narrate that poem of sorrow, anguish, and tears?

Voltaire opened wide his doors, at Ferney, to the mother and daughter of Sirven, and provided for the husband and father, who was in Geneva.

At the same time he wrote to Madame Calas and to her daughter in order to comfort them and make them hope for a speedy redress of their grievances. He protested with indignation against the assassination of young De la Barre, and stretched out his hand to the refugee D'Etallonde.

Voltaire interested all Protestant Europe in the fate of these persecuted families. To begin with, the sovereigns, Frederick, Christian VII., the king of Poland, and Catharine II., sent him donations for his clients.

"I believe I have told you," he writes to Damilaville on the 9th of February, 1767, "that the king of Denmark has just placed himself in the ranks of our benefactors. I have four kings in my hand, I must win the game. Do you not marvel at seeing how this life is made up of high and low, of white and black? and are you not sorry that, among our four kings, there is not one from the south?"

The mother of Sirven died with grief, and his wife gave birth to a dead child!

"You see," wrote Voltaire to D'Alembert, "what terrible misfortunes are caused by fanaticism."

But, as D'Alembert seemed to him altogether too impassive, he sent him the following reproachful letter:

"I cannot conceive how thinking beings can live in a nation of apes, where the apes become so often transformed into tigers. As for myself, I am ashamed to be even on the frontier. It is no longer time for jesting. Wit does not befit massacres. What! monsters in judges' gowns take amid the most horrid sufferings the lives of sixteen-year-old children! And the nation suffers it! Scarcely two words are spoken about it, then everybody runs off to the comic opera. I feel ashamed to show myself so sensitive and quick tempered at my age. But I mourn for those who have had their tongue torn out, while you use yours to say very agreeable and very pleasant things. You digest well, my dear philosopher, but I have a poor digestion. You are still young, and I am an old and a sick man. Forgive me this sadness."

During eight years, Voltaire, assisted by the celebrated advocate, Elie de Beaumont, struggled against the Parliament and the clergy in order to obtain a new trial of the Calas and Sirven suits.

"During that time," said he, "not an outburst of laughter escaped my lips with which I did not reproach myself as with a crime."

His generous exertions were finally crowned with success. The memory of Calas, whose innocence was acknowledged, was first of all rehabilitated by the Parliament of Toulouse; then Sirven, who had delivered himself up to his judges, was declared not guilty by the same Parliament.

In his enthusiasm Diderot wrote to Mlle. Voland: "It is Voltaire who pleads and writes for that unfortunate family. Oh, my friend, what a beautiful use of genius! That man must have a soul alive with sensibility to rebel as he does against injustice, and he must feel all the impulses of virtue. What are the Calases to him? What can interest him in their favor? What motive has he to interrupt the work he loves in order to undertake their defense? Were there a Christ, I assure you that Voltaire would be saved! . . ."

Voltaire again caused the rehabilitation of General Lally, whom a sentence of the Paris Parliament had sent to the hangman, and brought about a new trial of the suit brought against Montbailly and his wife, who had been sentenced to death by the judges of Arras under pretense of having murdered their mother, who had really died from apoplexy. Mont-

bailly was executed. The pregnancy of his wife
having postponed her execution, Voltaire was in time
to liberate her and rehabilitate the memory of her
husband.   He also obtained the rehabilitation of a
poor field laborer, Martin, accused of a murder, the
true author of which surrendered himself and con-
fessed the commission of the deed some time after
the execution of the innocent man.   Besides, by his
Request to all the Magistrates of the Kingdom, Voltaire pleaded and won against the canons of Saint-
Claude the cause of the serfs of Jura, those victims
of the mortmain.*

In a word, Voltaire, at Ferney, was the universal
advocate of right, the judge of the public conscience,
the great champion of justice and humanity.

It was not, however, without peril that the patriarch of Ferney executed his mission of redresser of
the iniquitous sentences rendered by the parliaments.
He was himself vehemently threatened by the Parliament of Paris.   This body had his books burned,
and the minister, duke of Choiseul, his protector,
said, " I will not be answerable for what the Parliament will do if Voltaire falls into its hands."

From all parts of France the unfortunate, the
oppressed, all who were molested in their freedom
of conscience, wrote to the patriarch of Ferney, or
came there to get from him support, advice, and
money.   And never did Voltaire refuse to any one
either money, counsel, or time.   Ferney had become a
kind of Mecca and Rome combined—the Mecca and
the Rome of Freethought.

---

*The term was then applied to conveyances of land made to
ecclesiastical bodies.

XVII.

In May, 1764, Voltaire wrote to Pastor Bertrand: "My dear philosopher, I have, thank God, broken all intercourse with kings. I know for the present no life but one of retirement with Madame Denis."

This was probably the faint echo of his last quarrel with Frederick about the Frankfort affair. But he could well say, "To be loved and to be free, these are the things that kings lack."

He was not as well cured of the kings as he wished to appear, and it was not long before he belied himself by beginning an exchange of letters with the empress of Russia, and writing to one of his friends: "I absolutely need a crowned head. I must have one at any price."

To the Alexander of the north he added the Semiramis of the north. A strange woman, a complex being, a hybrid, a veritable sphinx, was that empress, the murderess of her husband; a Messalina in her passions, yet cool as Minos, and with an unerring insight into great undertakings and state affairs. A superior organization was hers, and a mighty brain. Raising barbarous Russia to the rank of civilized nations, she became, at the same time, the mistress and the conqueror of a part of Poland and of almost the entire eastern empire. A great legislator, she was also a woman of letters, and, above all, a Freethinker and a friend of philosophers. Unable to have Voltaire at her court on account of his great age, which did not permit him to live on the banks of the Neva, she called to St. Petersburgh, Bernardin de St. Pierre, Ségur, and the Encyclopedists Grimm and Diderot.

In the middle of a conversation, as the latter fiery philosopher was developing his ideas with his usual free manner and crudity of expressions, he stopped short, fearing he had wounded the feelings of the empress as well as offended the woman. "Keep on, Mr. Diderot," quietly said Catharine, "*we are all men here.*"

She was indeed Catharine the Great. So she was called by Voltaire, who qualified her in turn as empress, Semiramis, and harlot.

In some letters from Catharine to the patriarch of Ferney, she seems constantly engrossed with the idea of paring the nails of the Russian Bear, of glossing his bristled hair, of dressing him, of bringing him nearer to the rest of civilized Europe, upon which she draws for teachers, male and female, savants, philosophers, and men of letters.

Voltaire overdid his adulation for the northern Semiramis so far as willingly to absolve her from the murder of her consort, Peter the third--a "*trifle; a family affair.*"

"I am her knight toward and against all," he wrote to Madame du Deffand. "I know very well she is reproached with some trifle about her husband, but these are private affairs with which I have nothing to do. . . . Besides, would Peter III. have done what she has done?"

Let us quote here a beautiful page of Jules Janin, who sketches one of the numerous phases of the many-sided Catharine. It was on the occasion of meeting, in one of her voyages, with the tumular stone of the unfortunate and immortal author of the *Metamorphoses,* who died in exile in Scythia, among the Sarmatians:.

"One day as she was walking about, dreaming of the future splendors of her unlimited dominions, the great Empress Catharine discovered, among some ruins, an abandoned tomb, and wanted to know who it was that rested under those briars. She was answered that it was a poet, a Roman, whose name was obliterated and forgotten. But she was a woman; she was the friend and disciple of Voltaire; she knew the history of her empire; and on that stone, worn out by time, she divined the name of Ovid. Then, in the midst of their journey through the deserts, a tear was seen dampening the eyes of this woman, who was little used to weeping. O sublime praise, eloquent, and thrice glorious tear! It is thus that at a distance of eighteen centuries this absolute woman-sovereign has washed away the wrong of that absolute despot, Augustus, emperor."

In his correspondence with Catharine, Voltaire does not spare genuflexions and worship. In a word, he was as much of a courtier toward her as he had been toward the king of Prussia. But he had his hours of free speech, when he said rough truths to the crowned heads, impelling them vigorously in the pathway of reason and progress. Besides, the reader must take good care not to judge Voltaire from the point of view of our nineteenth century, freed, as it has been, by the French Revolution. At the end of the previous age the crowned philosophers, the Fredericks and the Catharines, the Christians, the Josephs II., were the men who served as a shield for the Freethinker, the Encyclopedist, and, first of all, for Voltaire, against the roaring pack of Jesuits and clericals, the masters of France, and the despotic, bigoted, and corrupted court of Louis XV.,

who was but the tool of his confessors, and the puppet
of his mistress.

In answer to the furious attacks of the Jesuitical
party, the Nonottes and the Patouillets, the patriarch
of Ferney loved to say to Catharina: "I have on
my side, at least, the sovereign whose sway extends
over two thousand leagues of land. That consoles
me from the rogues. . . ."

Fell destroyer of the old world, Voltaire makes
everything subserve his purpose. The champion of
liberty, he uses royal and princely tools, which he
sharpens and bends at will. New Proteus, he
appears in every shape, even as a courtier around the
Pompadour, and about *Cotillon II.*, who, through his
influence and with the aid of Choiseul, will protect
the Encyclopedists and expel the Jesuits.

It is true, this great man sometimes stooped before
the powerful more than befitted a philosopher, but
it was really with the purpose of lifting up mankind;
of bringing it out of its darkness; of delivering it from
the chains that bound it; it was the better to *crush the
wretch*, as he styled the hydra of fanaticism. It is
true, he bowed before kings, but only on the condition that they became his instruments of progress—
harnessed themselves to his Freethinker's chariot and
established in their domain religious and political
tolerance.

"Philosophers have cringed long enough before
kings," said Frederick; "it is now the kings' turn to
cringe before philosophers."

Thus crowned heads rendered Voltaire's mission
and propaganda easy. Under their shield he was
able to make a fatal breach into the rampart of

error and superstition. It was through the kings he acted upon the nations.

If Voltaire sometimes sacrificed to forms and played the supple courtier, he never denied either his principles or personal opinions, even before or with respect to kings or emperors. When D'Alembert wrote him that the article on the Empress Catherina was about to appear in the *Encyclopedie,* asking him whether it would be advisable to insert what related to her private life and passion as well as to the murder of Peter III., Voltaire answered, "Tell the truth."

After a lapse of silence and mutual coldness, the correspondence with Frederick was once more renewed. The king wrote, "I believed you so taken up with crushing the wretch that I did not presume you would think of anything else."

Frederick seems, in this letter, to regret the *pique* at Berlin, with its consequences:

"You have preserved all the grace and amenity of your youth. You are the Prometheus of Geneva. If you had remained with us we would be something by this time. A fatality that presides over the things of this life has denied us so great an advantage," etc.

There arose no more misunderstandings between the two friends and philosophers. Frederick remained to the last faithful to the admiration with which Voltaire had inspired him in his youth. Indeed, he had been the very first, when yet crown prince of Prussia, to divine and appreciate the genius of Voltaire.

When Frederick knew that the Count of Falkenstein (Joseph II.) was in Paris and intended returning by way of Lyons and Switzerland, he wrote to the Count of Lamberg,

"I expect he will pass by Ferney, for he will desire to see and hear the man of the century, the Virgil and Cicero of our day."

But hearing that the emperor of Austria had passed Ferney without a word, the king looked upon that show of indifference as an insult to philosophy, and immediately wrote to D'Alembert:

"I hear that the Count of Falkenstein has seen numbers of arsenals, manufactures, ships, and seaports, but has not seen Voltaire. These other things are found everywhere, but to produce a Voltaire a century is necessary. Had I been in the emperor's place I should not have passed Ferney without waiting for the old patriarch, to be able to say at least that I had seen and heard him. I think a certain lady Theresa, a very poor philosopher, has forbidden her son to see the patriarch of tolerance."

Frederick had correctly surmised. It was Maria Theresa who had represented to her son that his visit to Ferney would be considered as an indorsement of the philosopher's irreligious doctrines. Joseph II., still under tutelage and merely a nominal emperor as yet, dared not disobey the maternal order, notwithstanding his eager desire to see the patriarch of Ferney, of whom he was the disciple, as he proved himself afterward.

The king of Denmark, Christian VII., at the time of his visit to the Count of Versailles, had been disagreeably surprised to find Voltaire detested and feared there. As he expressed his astonishment, they answered, "Voltaire has genius enough, but no religion!"

The patriarch of Ferney, who corresponded with the king of Denmark, addressed him an ode in which he congratulated him for his liberal administration and reforms, and severely criticised the censorship of the press in France, as can be seen from the following extract:

"The right to freely think thou dost to man restore,
And sermons, science, art, or fictions all may treat,
Whilst others hiss at will, or praise the author's lore;
The wings of Pegasus, alas, have been cropt here.
In Paris oft a clerk well up in formal phrase,
Does say to me: ' You must before my desk appear.
Without the king's consent how dare you think apace?
If you would air your wit, the king's police entreat.
The girls do so, and that without a thought of shame.
Their trade is well worth yours; is it not far more sweet?
We surely prize it much above your vaunted fame.' "

Voltaire wrote in prose or verse to king, prince, or empress, to the great as to the humble. He received not less than fifty letters a day, and not one remained without an answer, if we except, however, such as apostrophized him as a firebrand of hell, tool of Satan, or oldest son of his Plutonic majesty; all of which did not prevent his doing the honors of Ferney to the visitors who flocked to his hearth, and whose overflowing enthusiasm he knew how to reprove and quell by some pleasant stroke of wit. " I salute you, light of the world," said one of these." " Madame Denis," exclaimed Voltaire, " bring us a pair of snuffers."

Notwithstanding these corrections, he could not prevent those who came to see him from expressing their admiration.

A Flemish lady, Madame Suard, whom he had

known as a young girl, while in her native land,
wrote what follows, after a visit to Ferney:

"The sight, the conversation, of Voltaire are enchanting. There is not upon his face a trace, a furrow of age, that is not a charm."

To Madame Suard Voltaire seems almost divine.
Before leaving him she asked his blessing and kissed
his hands.

" Fortunately I am on the brink of the grave," said
the witty old man. " You would not treat me so if
I were but twenty."

"It was a sight," says the field-marshal, prince of
Ligny, " to behold him when animated by his beautiful and brilliant imagination, scattering wit by handfuls, imparting its sparkle to every one disposed to
understand and believe the beautiful and the good,
causing all to think and speak who were capable of it;
building houses for poor families, and good-natured
in his own interior, good-natured in his village, a
good-natured and a great man at the same time (bon-
homme et grand homme tout à la fois), a union without which a man is never completely either one or
the other, for genius gives extent to goodness, and
goodness to genius."

The prince of Ligny was right. The patriarch of
Ferney was not only the greatest mind, but also one
of the kindest hearts of his century.

The admiration which he inspired suggested to the
Parisians the idea of organizing a subscription for
raising a statue to him. Its execution was intrusted
to the sculptor, Pigale. Many foreigners having expressed their desire to subscribe themselves to the
Parisian initiative, the subscription became European.

Voltaire, meanwhile, rejected Jean Jacques Rousseau's subscription.

This statue was only finished in 1776. It is to-day in the library of the *Institut* with this dedication engraved on the pedestal: .

"To M. de Voltaire, from the men of letters, his compatriots and contemporaries, 1778."

XVIII.

All his household, and especially Madame Denis, urged Voltaire to go to Paris. He dreaded this voyage, and exclaimed:

"Go to Paris! but do you know there are in that city forty thousand fanatics who, with praises to heaven, would carry forty thousand fagots to build up a funeral pile for me? That would be my bed of honor!"

Notwithstanding, being persuaded by his niece, who was passionately fond of city life, he left Ferney on the 6th of February, 1778, to come and die in that very same year, decked with the flowers of his apotheosis, in Paris. He was received with universal rapture. The philosopher who had been all his life outside of France returned to the capital in triumph. The Parisian population nobly avenged on that day his long struggle against religious and political despotism, as well as the persecutions he had experienced.

"He comes, the defender of Calas! Vive Voltaire!" they cried, when he appeared in the streets, "He has been persecuted for fifty years!"

The academies went in a body to his hotel, as did also the consuls. The British ambassador left, marveling at having heard Voltaire speak a faultless English. The illustrious Franklin presented his grandson and asked Voltaire to bless him. Voltaire, resting his hands on the head of the child, pronounced these words : "GOD AND LIBERTY."

These two words, containing all the profession of faith of Voltaire, and summing up, so to speak, his life struggles, formed the charter of the American republic and were soon to become the watchword of the French Revolution.

The American patriarch and the patriarch of Ferney embraced each other with emotion. It seemed to the witnesses of the scene as if the old world and the new were come together in fraternal embrace.

From the genial enthusiasm which had declared itself on the arrival of Voltaire, it was clearly seen how rapid a progress his ideas had made, and how the revolution was already accomplished in the minds of men by the light he had projected and imparted to them, by the propagating power of his civilizing genius, beneath which the bastiles of the old regime crumbled one after another.

It may be that Louis XVI. had a presentiment of the danger, for he thought somewhat about expelling Voltaire from Paris, after his predecessor's example, and it was only upon the pressing entreaties of his young queen, Marie Antoinette, that he decided to authorize the philosopher's presence in the capital.

Voltaire could not leave his hotel without being surrounded and acclaimed.

"No," says a contemporary, "the apparition of a ghost, of a prophet, or even of an apostle, would not have produced more surprise and admiration that M. de Voltaire's arrival."

Age had made him lose nothing of his ironical *verve.*

When he had entered the city by the gate of Fontainebleau, the custom officers having asked him whether he had anything liable to duty, Voltaire answered, "Gentlemen, I am the only contraband article here."

One day, when his carriage was surrounded by an enthusiastic crowd which obstinately pursued him with its acclamations, the councilor of state, M. Elos, who was also in the carriage, said to him, " Yet, all these people are here to do you homage."

" Yes," replied Voltaire, " but were I being led to the scaffold there would be a great many more of them."

His change of location brought on a severe indisposition, which gratified the enemies of the sage of Ferney to such a degree that all the pious gazettes printed, with an ill-disguised joy, these welcome words, *Voltaire is dying* (*Voltaire se meurt*).

A large number of people went to his hotel and left their names in token of sympathy; others, in spite of the peremptory prohibition of M. Tronchin, his physician, forced their way to the sick man, surrounded his bedside, and wearied him out. He grew worse, and began to spit blood. Mme. Denis sent for the Abbé Gautier and introduced him. It has been asserted that Voltaire made a formal retraction of his principles to him. The reality of the imputation is more than doubtful, and it is contradicted by a note which Voltaire left with his secretary Wagnière. The note read thus:

"I die worshiping God, loving my friends, not hating my enemies, and detesting superstition."

   ("Signed)   VOLTAIRE."

"February 28, 1778."

Nevertheless, the nervous vitality with which Voltaire was endowed triumphed over his malady. Scarcely out of his bed of sickness, he takes up anew his work with his usual feverish activity. *Irene* is played on the 16th of May. At the sixth representation of this tragedy, the Parisian gave him a veritable apotheosis, a triumph in truly antique fashion. The Theatre Français was surrounded by a crowd which acclaimed Voltaire as soon as he appeared, with his great peruke and long sleeves of point lace, together with the magnificent sable furs of which Catherine II. had made him a present.

Within, the audience packed, crammed the theater to its utmost capacity. When Voltaire entered he was greeted, overwhelmed with flowers and bravos. The ladies, standing up in their boxes, frantically applauded him; and the acclamations did not even end with the piece, which had scarcely been listened to, notwithstanding the efforts of the poet, who tried in vain to arrest the impetuous tide of enthusiasm, as he wept with joy and cried out, "Would you then have me die with pleasure and smother beneath your blossoms !"

From the green-room the bust of Voltaire was brought upon the stage and covered with crowns and garlands amid a storm of plaudits. Mme. Vestris (Irene) then advanced to the footlights and read the following verses, written by the marquis of Saint Marc:

Before rejoicing Paris, here,
Receive this day an homage true,
Which after ages, though severe,
Can but confirm and join in, too.
Thou need'st not cross beyond grim death's uncertain bound
Before thou dost enjoy sweet immortality.
Voltaire, accept this crown ;
It is thy due to-day;
A glorious gift 'tis to receive,
When France deems it a joy to give !

Mme. Vestris repeated this rather mediocre piece, which, however, was greeted with frantic transports, and, *nolens volens*, Voltaire had to submit and allow himself to be crowned. They decked his head with laurels; the enthusiasm knew no bounds. Voltaire, exhausted, retires. The crowd opens to let him pass. But every one wants to approach him, to touch him, to kiss his hands, to hear him speak a single word. Along the street, his carriage is surrounded, stopped, and the throng endeavor to unhitch the horses in order to carry him in triumph. Everywhere the cry is heard, *Vive Voltaire!* At last the coachman succeeds in disengaging the vehicle and saving his master from the dangerous pressure of the delirious crowd.

"Envy and hatred," says Grimm, after this unprecedented triumph, "dared to growl only in secret; and for the first time, perhaps, public opinion in France was seen to enjoy full and undisputed sway."

Voltaire, although on the brink of the tomb, did not cease either to think or labor. On the 2d of April, 1778, he is received as a member by the Masonic lodge of the Neuf Sœurs (Nine Sisters). A few days after, he persuades the Academie Française to publish a dictionary upon a new plan, himself taking charge of the letter *A.*

"I thank you in the name of the alphabet," said Voltaire on leaving the learned assembly.

"And we thank you in the name of *letters,*" replied the chevalier de Chastelux.

Voltaire goes again to the Theatre Français to witness the representation of his *Alzire.* New acclamations and plaudits. "He attends the sessions of the Academy of Sciences; he stops only when worn-out nature refuses longer to follow this vigorous and indefatigable mind. It is in vain he uses coffee and abuses it; his stomach will not perform its work any longer. On the 20th of May, attacked with strangury, he took to his bed, fell in a kind of torpor, and ten days after, the 30th of May, 1778, expired at the mansion of the Marquis de Villette, on the quay of the Théatins, to-day called Quai Voltaire. He had attained the age of eighty-four years, three months, and ten days. His birth had been at Châtenay, near Sceaux, on the 20th of February, 1694.

To his very last breath Voltaire was animated with the spirit of justice. Four days before his death he seemed to come to life again on learning through the son of Lally-Tollendal of his father's rehabilitation. This was one of the cases taken hold of and pleaded by the patriarch of Ferney. He wrote to Lally the following letter (the last he ever penned), which seems worthily to crown his life of struggle for the right:

"The dying man returns to life on learning this happy news. He tenderly embraces M. de Lally. He sees the king is the friend of justice; he will die content."

It is useless to mention the filthy inventions through which the Catholic writers have tried to sully the memory of Voltaire by representing his death-agony as that of a repenting sinner. The truth is that he repelled the services of the Abbé L'Attaignant, saying, "Let me die in peace." He is reported to have answered the curate of Saint-Sulpice, who exhorted him to invoke Jesus Christ, "In the name of God, do not speak of that man to me." At the last stage of his agony he addressed these words to M. Morand, "Adieu, my dear Morand; I am dying."

Seven years before, Voltaire had written to the king of Prussia:

"I do not fear death, which approaches apace; but I have an unconquerable aversion for the manner in which we have to die in our holy, Catholic, apostolic, and Roman religion. It seems to me extremely ridiculous to have myself oiled to depart to the other world as we grease the axles of our wagons before a trip. This stupidity and all that follows is so repugnant to me that I am tempted to have myself carried to Neufchâtel to have the pleasure of dying within your dominions."

In November, 1777, he again wrote Frederick on the same subject, as follows:

"I am to-day eighty-four years old. I have more aversion than ever for extreme unction and those who administer it."

The remains of Voltaire, although he had expired without the sacraments of the church, were, notwithstanding his expressed wish to be buried in Ferney, transported to the abbey of Scelliéres (Episcopal See of Troyes, about eighty miles nearly southeast of

Paris), by the order of his nephew, the Abbé Mignot, and interred in the center of the nave. The bishop of Troyes had forbidden the prior to proceed with the interment and to have a religious service, but the Episcopal prohibition had arrived too late.

Through a last irony of fate, the enemy of the church was buried in consecrated ground and in her very bosom.

Before this present centenary year (1878), the memory of the great philosopher had already received many public homages. The first came from the king of Prussia, Frederick, who on the 26th of November, 1778, read before the Academy of Sciences and Belles-Lettres of Berlin a *Eulogy of Voltaire*, written at the camp of Schatlzar.

In 1779 the Academie Française listened to a triple encomium on Voltaire delivered respectively by Ducis (who inherited his chair in the Academy), D'Alembert, and the abbé of Radouviliers.

Voltaire having been the motor, the powerful impulse, of the new world of ideas and principles which expressed and materialized itself in the French Revolution, it was natural for his legitimate offspring and child to give a signal testimonial of its filial gratitude to his memory. The National Assembly voted the removal of his ashes to the Pantheon. They were accordingly taken from the abbey of Scelliéres and transferred to Paris on the 11th of July, 1791. The National Assembly, the municipal officers, the State bodies, and a multitude whose acclamations in honor of their heroic champion were not quelled even by this renewed national sorrow, followed the casket to the vaults of the Pantheon.

In 1822 the remains of Voltaire and Rousseau

were clandestinely taken from the Pantheon and thrown in the gutter by the jesuitic Restoration.

Even beyond the tomb has the church, conscious of the mortal wound she received at the hands of Voltaire, pursued him with her hatred and her vengeance. But if she threw Voltaire's ashes to the wind, she has been herself unable to prevent the Voltairian ideas from instilling themselves and breathing life into the minds of this, our own age, to-day celebrating the anniversary of the great philosopher of the eighteenth century.

THE WORK OF VOL-
TAIRE.

XIX.—THE WORK OF VOLTAIRE.

After La Harpe, Palissot, Duvernet, Villemain, Pierre Leroux, Sainte-Beuve, Philarète Chasles, Nisard, Desnoireterre, Arsène Houssaye, David Frederick Strauss, it may seem superfluous to attempt anew an appreciation of the genius and great faculties of Voltaire. In the following concise terms, he has been most admirably painted by the eloquent pen of Goethe: "Genius, imagination, depth, extent, reason, taste, philosophy, elevation, originality, naturalness, wit and the graces of wit, variety, accuracy, finesse, warmth, charm, grace, force, information, vivacity, preciseness, clearness, elegance, eloquence, gayety, ridicule, pathos, and truth, that is Voltaire. He is the French writer *par excellence.*"

Goethe has also said :

"It is not astonishing to learn that Voltaire secured to himself, uncontested, the universal empire over the minds of Europe.

"Voltaire will ever be regarded as the greatest man of literature in modern times, and perhaps even in all times; as the most astonishing creation of the author of nature, a creation in which he has been pleased to unite at once, in the frail and perilous organization of man, all the varieties of talent, all the glories of genius, all the potencies of thought."

Who has not read Voltaire? Who ignores that throughout the seventy volumes that make up his literary work he steadily pursues the same end, that is, to clean out the stables of Augeas, to drive away the darkness of ignorance from the mind of man, to break the shackles of superstition, to disperse the phantoms that would haunt his perplexed brain, in a word, to give him his intellectual compass?

The works of Voltaire are an immortal monument raised up to human progress, reason, justice, and common sense. They are all pervaded with a passionate love of the just and the true.

In his *Essay Upon the Morals and Mind of Nations*, in his *Charles XII.*, and in the *Age of Louis XIV.*, he renovates history; throughout the march of events he seeks to retrace the Odyssey of the human mind. In his *Philosophical Dictionary* he creates the power of criticism, he proclaims the independence of all moral law from superstition or religious creed, he lifts up human kind from its kneeling posture before the idols of divine right.

In his classical drama he is still pursuing his polemical warfare; he pleads tolerance, and the horror of fanaticism and superstition. In his philosophical novels he quizzes and finally tears to shreds the yet triumphant absurdities and prejudices, the errors of his age, the false systems *à la* Pangloss.* He charms and instructs at the same time, lavishing on his reader the sparkling flowers of his wit.

"I do not see," says M. Taine, "in what idea the man would be wanting who had as his breviary the

---

*Pangloss, preceptor of Candide, the hero of *Candide or Optimism*, taught the " metaphysico-theologo-cosmolo-block-headology," and held that all was " for the best in this best of worlds."

Dialogues, the *Dictionary*, and the novels of Voltaire."

To the silly, ridiculous, distorted humanity he had before him, Voltaire offered the noble image of the ideal humanity, which he carried within him. By his writings, illuminated with the flashes of his mind and the fire of his genius, he threw the *sursum corda* to the generations of his time, and succeeded in setting them upon their feet by steadying them against the immovable pillar of liberty, truth, and reason.

What is, after all, more important to bring to light than the words of Voltaire is the *work* of Voltaire, his individuality, the influence of his ideas upon his times, upon the Europe of the eighteenth century.

During more than a half century, and up to his very death at the age of eighty-four years, Voltaire held the intellectual and moral scepter of Europe. In contrast with Fontenelle* he opens wide his hands and scatters truth broadcast in every fashion—through his eloquence, his admirable writings, his witty conversation, and no less witty correspondence, in which he reveals himself in all the brightness of his good sense, unequaled genius, and passionate love for humanity. The Vulcan of mind and truth, he hammers out those keen darts, those curt and palpitating sentences, that would have pierced the skin of a hippopotamus, and with them ran the cuirass of fanaticism through and through.

To formulate his ideas, to draw up his code of common sense, to render his judgments and shape

---

*Bernard de Fontenelle, poet and philosopher, 1657–1754.

the public conscience and opinion, Voltaire finds an
idiom as luminous as a sun ray, as clear as a crystal
spring reflecting the azure sky in its pure and tranquil bosom; he creates that admirable French tongue
which since his time has been so poorly spoken and
written, spoiled as it has been by the adjunct of
heavy and discordant tinsel.

In the midst of a discussion, some *quidam* having
spoken ironically of the fine and grand sentences of
Voltaire, the latter quickly replied, "My fine sentences ! . . . Know sir, that I have never made
one."

Voltaire was then the indefatigable pioneer of
Freethought. He broke over all intellectual bar-
riers, pulled down with a strong hand all the worm-
eaten hulks of the past, the superannuated dogmas,
the political and religious jails. With strokes of axe
and pick he cleared up the inextricable forest of
errors and prejudices, and opened out a straightfor-
ward and free highway for the human caravan. He
impudently laughed in the face of all the nonsense of
past and present, laughed with the sparkling and
withering laughter we know him by. With a sarcastic
word, with a single ironical shaft, Voltaire ruined an
established system. The exaggerated optimism of
Leibnitz crumbled beneath the single aphorism of
Dr. Pangloss in his *Candide*: "All is for the best in
this best of possible worlds."

After sketching the bloody and dismal Odyssey of
departed generations, Voltaire exclaimed, "It seems
as if the history of man had been written by the
hand of the executioner !"

But, spite of the dark pages of history, Voltaire
asserted his faith in progress by this witty axiom,

"Truth is the child of time, and her father must sooner or later allow her to go into society " (la laisser aller dans le monde).

This great philosopher so well understood the civilizing necessities and the interests of that Europe of which he was the most illustrious representative, that he wrote the following very sound aphorism, over which certain diplomats of our day might do well to meditate: "Every war between Europeans is a civil war."

To appreciate the merit, difficulty, and greatness of Voltaire's work, it is necessary to remember that he lived in a period when the books of Freethought were burned by the executioner's hand; when, Freethinkers were led to the scaffold, to the pile, or suffered banishment; when the Spanish Inquisition still made *autos da fé* with heretics; when did not exist the liberty of conscience any more than the liberty of the press; in a word, when political and religious barbarism reigned over Europe.

Now we shall see what consequences, what happy results were accomplished by Voltaire's apostolate, and how that powerful genius transformed the barbarism of Europe into civilization.

Thanks to the incessant harangues and superhuman efforts of this ever active tribune, the minds of men are electrified, the current of ideas is checked and turned in an opposite direction.

Through the influence of Voltaire, the great Frederick, in Prussia, establishes and promotes religious tolerance, free thought, and scientific activity. We must seek nowhere else the secret of the powerful and rapid development of Prussia. On the day when Frederick II. gave her the liberty to think, and encouraged science by the foundation of academies, by the pensioning of savants and lettered men, by every possible means he created its strength and prepared her future triumph.

Following the example of the Prussian king, the most of the petty princes of Germany, as also the kings of Denmark, Sweden, Poland, and Joseph II., emperor of Austria, allow in their realms free research and freedom of thought and expression. The inquisition was abolished in Spain.

Still through Voltaire's influence, the empress Catherine abolishes torture and decrees tolerance in her vast empire. In France, the cases against Calas, Sirven, Lally, Montbailly, are reinvestigated, the judgments reversed and their memory rehabilitated.

Thus is a man of genius capable of accomplishing great results. Thus he may spur along, teach, and transform his age, when his name is Voltaire.

What makes this most astonishing, is that this Hercules, who bore the new world upon his powerful shoulders, was almost constantly ill. He found consolation for his precarious health in saying, "The puppets of Providence cannot last as long as she."

And he wrote to the count d'Argental:

"I gambol every day over my grave. Life is a child we have to rock until it falls asleep."

On an anniversary of the Saint Bartholomew, he was taken with a violent fever, which was accelerated and increased by the profound indignation with which the execrated memory of the great Catholic massacre inspired him.

"It is the Furies of the Saint Bartholomew, the *Dragonnades*, and the war of the Albigenses,"

Strauss has said, "which in Voltaire brandish their torches against Christianism."

From what source did this valetudinarian draw his indefatigable activity, his ever-renewing ardor, his invincible strength? He drew them from the sentiment of justice and intense love for humanity.

Of Voltaire it can truly be said that nothing that is human was foreign to him. Every outrage, every violence, every wound inflicted on humanity, he felt within himself; he resented and avenged them!

Henry Heine has said of the author of Faust and Werther, "When nature wished to recognize and admire herself, she created Goethe." In the same manner, when the genius of humanity would have the consciousness of its strength and its splendor, it created Voltaire, and built him of sensibility, common sense, wit, and judgment, kneaded together through and through.

Neither Montesquieu, Rousseau, nor Diderot, great as they were, had the intellectual power and universality of Voltaire. Neither of them has weighed so heavily in the scale of his respective age. Voltaire stands as the central and immovable pillar of Freethought, which no religious reaction will either beat down or pass. The most violent tides of obscurantism have beaten themselves again, and expired in impotent rage at the foot of his statue. The formidable influence of Voltaire upon his own epoch has been continued into ours, and it is in part to this still active power we owe the great springs of our civilization, the idea of progress, the definitive triumph over religious intolerance, the liberty of conscience, boons which will not be torn away from us, whatever the enemies of progress may do.

What is worthy of our admiration in the eighteenth century, is the ardent love of liberty and the frankness of expression of those who fight in the arena of Freethought. How nimble and sprightly they are! They feel they bear within themselves the destinies of humanity and the gestation of a revolution of thought. Reproducing the heroic energy, the contempt for danger of the valiant group of the thinkers of the sixteenth century (De la Boétie, Pierre Charron, Rabelais, Montaigne), they do not hesitate, they never erase, but go straight to their aim and to the fact. They call a cat a cat, a priest a hypocrite, and the obscurantists consummate rascals. In this they have set a great example for our age of tergiversation, happy means, and delicate equivocations, which eclecticism, in a compromise with clericalism, has kept in bonds and retarded during a space of almost fifty years.

The eighteenth century had the good fortune to find in Voltaire its man, its expression, and its interpreter, a good fortune which has not fallen to our nineteenth century, still so troubled, drawn hither and thither, muddled, priest-ridden, and hesitating between progress and tradition, authority and freedom, the revolution and counter-revolution, science and religion, faith and common sense, and actually in the condition of Buridan's ass between two measures full of oats.

Perhaps all our century lacks to bring order to its chaos and light up its torch, is simply a *fiat lux*, a living encyclopedia, a synthetic, clear, and powerful genius like Voltaire. Not a thinker of our age has felt his shoulders strong enough to don the armor of that knight of reason. No man is now giant

enough to undertake and carry through sixty years
of such a merciless and deadly warfare as Voltaire
led against the spirit of darkness. He was the or-
chestra leader, the goad, the impressario and director
of that valiant band of living Encyclopedists who
neither put water in their wine nor ambiguous words
in their sentences. He was, in short, king Voltaire;
a king without a realm, a king of the mind, perpetu-
ally driven from France by the wretches whe waxed
fat on the credulity and servileness of men who
did not intend to have the springs of their revenue
dried up by the truths of a philosopher. He so riddled
the intolerants with epigrams, so ridiculed their absurd doctrines, so worried the wretch and the
wretches, as he said; he threw such floods of
light into the dark recesses where the chains of slavery were forged; he so transfixed with his pointed
arrows the monster of fanaticism and despotism that
the bleeding and furious bull came and threw itself
headlong upon the avenging sword of the French
Revolution!

This memorable and most fruitful revolution
had been clearly predicted by Voltaire in his letter
dated April 2, 1764, and addressed to the Marquis
de Chauvelin:

"All that I see scatters the seed of a revolution
which will inevitably take place, and which I shall
not have the pleasure of witnessing. The French progress slowly in everything, but they progress. The
light has spread from man to man in such a degree
that at the first opportunity it will break out, and
then there will be a noisy time. Our young men
are fortunate. They will see some beautiful things!"

VOLTAIRE'S PROPA-
GANDISM.

XX. —VOLTAIRE'S PROPAGANDISM.

Voltaire accelerated the gestation of that great revolution which he announced and felt near at hand during the last year of his life not only by his own writings but also by the editing and publication of the works of others whenever they seemed to him useful productions. Having heard of the philosophical testament of Meslier, curé of Etrépigny, in the Department of Ardennes, he wrote in 1735 to Thiérot :

"Who can this village curé be of whom you speak? What! a curé, and a French curé at that, as much of a philosopher as Locke? Could you not send me the manuscript? I would faithfully return it to you."

But not until 1762 did Voltaire succeed in securing the testament of Meslier, a production we must consider as the first prelude to the Revolution. Voltaire published thousands upon thousands of copies. Criticising its "horse-cart" style and tedious details, he gave only a number of extracts from it. But later the work appeared entire.

According to his prudent custom, Voltaire hastened to protest against the publication of the book he had edited. In 1763 he wrote to D'Alembert the following letter, meant to be hawked around:

"There has been printed in Holland the *Testament* of Jean Meslier; it is only a portion of that curé's testament. I was filled with horror as I read it. The testimony of a priest who on his death-bed asks God's forgiveness for having taught the Christian religion may throw a great weight in the scale of the libertines. I will send you a copy of this *Testament* of the antichrist, since you want to refute it. It is written with a coarse simplicity which, unfortunately, looks like candor."

But some time afterward he wrote:

"It seems to me that the *Testament* of Jean Meslier is producing more effect; all who read it remain convinced; that man discusses and proves. He speaks at the moment of death, a moment when liars tell the truth; that is the strongest argument. . . . Jean Meslier must convert the world. Why is his gospel in so few hands?"

And Voltaire took good care to multiply the editions, which were rapidly taken up. But it was not idle in him to defend himself against the production of a book so essentially revolutionary, and which sapped at once the walls of royalty and of the church. Its effect was immense, and there is no doubt that it hastened the fall of the royal and clerical despotism.

After having passed the greater part of a modest and virtuous existence in Étrépigny, in Ardennes, where he had a crow to pick with the archbishop of Rheims, who maltreated and robbed the peasants, Meslier left, in 1729, the year of his death, a political and religious testament of 366 pages, registered in the court records of Saint Menehould, Department of Marne. In 1793 Anacharsis Clotz proposed to the Convention the erection of a monument to the Abbé Meslier, the first priest who had the courage and loyalty to abjure religious error.

The curé of Etrépigny sees in the multiplicity of religions on the earth the conclusive proof of their common falseness. Each of them, he says, proclaims itself the only true one and claims divine origin; but all cannot be true and divine, since they contradict each other on so many points, and mutually antagonize as well as damn each other. All religions, the Roman Catholic like all others, are the work of men, and the fact that they all pretend to divine origin shows them to rely and build upon an imposture primarily invented by designing leaders, then improved upon and developed by impostors and false prophets, eagerly accepted by human ignorance, and used by the great and the powerful of earth as a scarecrow for the masses. If a God, infinitely wise and good, had thought it necessary to reveal a religion, he would have rendered all error, all negation, impossible by impressing it with the unmistakable signs of its divinity. Since no religion bears these marks, all being open and vulnerable to negation and contestation, it follows that none is the result of divine revelation. The proof of the imposture of all religions is found, besides, in their foundation, *faith*, that is a certainty without proofs, forbidding discussion and denouncing the light of reason and researches of science as crimes against the Divinity. Far from being a source of truth, faith is only a source of error, illusion, and fraud. The Christian religion has vainly sought to draw proofs of the truth of its doctrines from miracles, themselves requiring proof; from her martyrs, who, according to their own co-religionists' avowals, irrationally sought a useless death; and from prophecies recorded in the holy scriptures, the very book needing proof of its genuineness and divine origin.

According to the priest Meslier, these hypotheses, webs of error, fables, and contradictions, are deserving of no credence. The stories of Eden and of the serpent, the history of the prophets, the Old and the New Testaments, the gospel, with its vulgar parables, do not come up to the fables of Æsop, and are far below the works of heathenish antiquity. The so-called sacred books are the production of ignorant and coarse minds.

Meslier pitilessly rails at the belief of Christianity, at the absurd doctrine of the trinity, according to which one is three and three are one; he keenly derides the biblical stories, the God of the Old Testament, who, like any other man, talks with Adam, walks around the garden of Eden with him, and finally damns him for having tasted of the fruit of the tree of knowledge and for having foolishly eaten, together with Eve, of the apple of damnation.

The curé of Etrepigny asks himself how God ever could have interested himself in such an insignificant and unworthy tribe as the Jews, to whom he promises supremacy over all other nations.

Under a sense of humiliation and regret for having been obliged to teach the divinity of the son of Mary and the carpenter Joseph, the cure of the Ardennes avenges himself by incisive criticisms of that pretended savior's mission. This so-called God, he says, has had all the weaknesses, all the passions of men, as is attested by his relations with the courtesan, Mary Magdalene, who was possessed of devils. This thaumaturgist, who heals a few sick Jews, has allowed all the ills and pests of humanity to remain after him. Jesus has simply been made the object and excuse of an apotheosis, after the model of ancient divinities, "of illustrious men and women, princes and princesses, for instance, or other persons of distinction who have arrogated to themselves, or to whom ignorance, servility, or flattery have applied the name of god or goddess."

Contradicting the deism of Voltaire, and going much farther than he, the cure Meslier denies the creating principle. "What is gained," he asks, "by the hypothesis of such a being? I see motions and forms, the phenomena of nature, which fill me with astonishment. Shall I have a better conception of them when I have invented a being who will have endowed her with these peculiarities? Besides, God, a perfect being, can never have created a world so imperfect, so filled with suffering and misery, a world made up of a mixture of good and evil. This heterogeneous admixture proves that no such being exists. Being is simply a phenomenon of matter."

Meslier denies a future life, and holds the life of men and animals to be nothing more than a kind of fermentation of the matter of which they are constituted. Sensation and thought are only special and limited modifications of that perpetual modification or fermentation called life; at death the process comes to an end, and what we call soul becomes extinguished as does the light of an exhausted candle. As for an existence beyond our mundane sphere, it is simply an invention of the priests, who make it the means of domineering over humanity, to live idly and uselessly on the honey and fat of the land, and therefore exert themselves in offering to the credulous an eternal

felicity in a fantastic paradise, while awing their imagination by fears of the endless torments of an
imaginary hell.

Our Ardennese curate was no less bold and radical
on the political than on the religious question. He
begins by criticising the attitude of the church
toward the state and its abuses.

" A religion," says Meslier, " that tolerates abuses
contrary to justice and natural equity, and therefore
contrary to the proper government of men and injuri-
ous to the public good, a religion that approves and
authorises these abuses and even indorses tyranny or
the tyrannical government of earthly kings or princes,
cannot be a true religion."

In his *Age of Louis XIV.*, Voltaire had sketched
the brilliant sides and happy influences of a reign
which patronized genius and allowed civilizing ideas
to shine and spread their rays about. Meslier, on
the contrary, shows us the shadows of the *sun-king* *
and the frightful misery caused by absolute monarchy.

"Do you wonder, O unhappy nations," said he,
" how it is you have to struggle with many difficulties and bear so much suffering in this life? It is
because you carry alone all the heaviness and weight
of labor and heat, just as the laborers spoken of in a
parable of the gospel; it is because you are laden,
you and your like, with all the monk tribe, the legal
pack, the soldiering hosts, the excise bands, the
swarming gatherers of salt and tobacco tax, in a word
with all the lazy and useless species in the world.

Louis XIV. has been poetically called *le roi-soleil*, the sun-
king.

For it is only with the fruits of your painful labor that such people live, as well as of all the kind, male and female, that serve them. You furnish through your work all that is necessary for their existence; more even, all that can minister to their recreation and pleasures."

And farther on:

"They speak to you about the evil one; they frighten you with the mere name of the devil because they want to have you believe that devils are the most wicked, mean, and frightful of beings. But our painters deceive themselves when on their canvas they represent devils as monsters frightful to see; they deceive themselves, I say, and deceive you, as also do your sermonizers, when in their pictures or sermons they make them appear to you so homely, hideous, and misshapen. They should rather, both painters and preachers, represent them to you as these fine grandees and nobles all, as these fine ladies and young damsels whom you see so well tricked up, so well dressed, curled, and scented, and so dazzling with gold, silver, and precious stones. The devils which your preachers and painters sketch for you and represent under such homely and monstrous forms and countenance, are certainly no more than imaginary devils, who could only frighten children or ignorant boors, and who could only inflict imaginary evil on those who bear them. But these he and she devils, these ladies and fine gentlemen of whom I speak to you, are certainly not imaginary, they are really visible, they must assuredly know how to inspire fear, and the evil they do to the poor is most, undeniably real and palpable."

After this the curate handles the topic of social conditions and of the complicity of princes and priests in maintaining their social despotism:

"All men are equal by nature," says Meslier; "they have all an equal right to live and inhabit the earth, an equal right to enjoy upon it their national liberty and to share of the fruits of the earth by usefully laboring to obtain the things necessary and useful to life. As they live in societies, it is absolutely necessary there should be among men interdependence and subordination. But this dependence and subordination should be just and fairly adjusted; that is, they should not tend to elevate the one too highly while lowering the other too much, nor to favor the one while crushing the others, nor to give all to the first and nothing to the rest, nor lastly, to place all possession and pleasure on one side and all burdens, cares, sorrows, and hardship on the other. Religion, we might think, should condemn the harshness and injustice of a tyrannical regime, just as we might expect, on the other side, to see a wise political science put a curb on the errors and abuses of a false religion. Certainly it should be. Yet it is not thus. State and religion have a mutual understanding and work into each other's hands, as do two accomplices. The priests recommend obedience to the authority of princes, whom they represent as being chosen of God; the princes, in return, uphold the functions of the clergy and furnish them with revenue. It is necessary, then, to fight both evils. All nations should unite and forget whatever quarrels may divide them in order to shake off the yoke which, with the help of tyrants and clergy, princes and nobles have imposed upon the people. All nations should combine and forget all differences of a nature to alienate them in order to work in common at this truly useful and necessary task, the annihilation of the monsters who enslave and oppress them."

Would it not seem as if Diderot had paraphrased this passage of Meslier in his famous dithyramb:

"And with his hands he would the bowels of the priest,
In lack of cord, entwine and twist to strangle kings."

But the curé of Etrépigny thinks it is best to begin with the church and religion, which keep in their leading strings the intellect and soul of the masses and dissuade nations from resisting tyrannical governments.

In a word, the priest who sounds the tocsin of the Revolution looks upon human kind as mystified, deceived by priests and oppressed by tyrants. In his eyes all religions are founded on imposture, all governments on a system of brigandage, arbitrariness, and oppression.

Thorough and vigorous logician in his political and religious criticism, Meslier is weaker when the question is to reconstruct the ruined social edifice. The advocate of communistic association, he imagines that all the inhabitants of a city, parish, or village should form an only family, consider each other as brothers and sisters, parents and children, and consequently partake in common of the same food, wear the same garb, dwell in similar houses, and distribute labor in common according to need or talent. The neighboring communities should form alliances among them, by which they would bind themselves to treat each other with kindness and justice, to lend each other assistance, etc.

Such is, in a concise way, the will and testament of the curé Meslier; such is this forerunner of the Revolution of '89, which, although shorn at first of its political portion, had Voltaire for its propagator and first editor.

PHILOSOPHICAL SYSTEM OF VOLTAIRE.

XXI. —THE PHILOSOPHICAL SYSTEM OF VOLTAIRE.

The eighteenth century was neither sentimental nor greatly metaphysical. "*It is brain I have here*," said Mme. de Tencin,* as she placed her hand upon her heart. Her words express quite fairly the moral state of the eighteenth century. In metaphysics it has remained non-committal. Possessed of too much intelligence to feed on the great empty words which have been the chief pabulum of our pedantic and puffed-up age, decisive and unequivocal in their affirmations and negations, the philosophers of the eighteenth century showed no particular taste for the fussy passages at arms now in vogue, in which existence and non-existence, absolute and contingent, subjective and objective, origin of matter, final causes, transcendent and unknowable, and such bombastic terms, are like tremendous projectiles thrown from the philosophical mortars, to rise and fall reciprocally upon the heads of the several contestants, with no other result than to leave the world in greater ignorance and confusion upon the principles involved than before their wordy warfare had begun. Voltaire loved to rail at these abstract speculators, saying that whenever two interlocutors ceased to understand each other it was because they were talk-

---

* Claudine de Tencin, 1681–1749, born in Grenoble, woman of the world, writer of several novels and friend of Fontenelle.

ing metaphysics. "And what are the romances of our unreliable imagination worth in these inaccessible questions?" he would exclaim.

What is attractive about the eighteenth century is precisely the sincerity of its doubts, the frankness of its skepticism, its love of clearness and horror of the nebulous. It seeks for truth, but failing to find it declares without equivocation that there are bounds for human knowledge. Its greatest thinkers were subject to frequent metaphysical shiftings. Diderot had begun with deism, to ground himself at last in pantheism, or rather in naturalism. His creative mind animated matter and made it the concrete expression of the forces, probabilities, and forms of being.

One day, a friend surprising him absorbed in meditation in the middle of a solitary wood, slipped up to him and touched him on the shoulder, and asked, "What are you doing here, Diderot?" "I am listening," he answered.

Diderot thought that with his monads, Leibnitz had no use for a God. With this restriction he was a follower of Leibnitz and a believer in monads.

For him nature was, after all, but a grand and single being, becoming self-conscious in the brain of man. It is very nearly Hegel's theory and his infinite manifested through the human mind.

In spite of his sallies against metaphysics, Voltaire constantly interested himself in the great questions of God, the soul, thought, free will. In contrast with Diderot, he had begun with Spinozism. After having wandered for some time on the vast ocean of matter, he had returned to deism.

He draws his first proof of God from social utility.

"This sublime system," says he, in his poem to the author of the *Three Impostors*,

> " This sweet, sublime belief is needful to our race;
> It is the sacred bond of our society;
> The first foundation of celestial equity,
> The curb of evil men, the hope of all the just.
> If heaven e'er, despoiled of a most sacred trust,
> Could cease to manifest a God and honor him,
> If God were not, we must invent and worship him."

Voltaire founds his belief in God principally on the cosmological argument. Something exists; therefore something has existed from all eternity (Voltaire, in spite of himself, falls into pantheism here). The world is built with intelligence, therefore it has been created by an intelligence, by the Great Architect of the universe. The movements of heavenly bodies, the gravitation of our globe around the sun, are subject to and accomplished through laws of mathematical exactness. Either the stars are themselves great geometers or else they are the work of the great geometer, in accordance with Plato's definition. In a dialogue in the *Philosophical Dictionary* a philosopher asks of Nature how, so rugged and silent in the mountain, she appears so industrious in its animals and trees. "My poor child," answers she, "shall I tell the truth? They have given me a name that does not fit me. They call me Nature, and I am all art." A work of art implies, necessarily, creation. God's nature is action; he has ever acted, and the world is an eternal emanation of his person. (Here we land in Brahmanism and Buddhism.)

According to Spinoza, God is the whole of everything; according to Voltaire, on the contrary, everything springs from God: "From the Supreme Being,

oternal and intelligent, spring in all time all beings
and all forms of being in space." Thus he approaches
Spinoza, but he differs from him again by his notions
of finality which the Amsterdam philosopher rejected
in his ideas of nature.

To Voltaire, therefore, there exists a creative intelligence from all eternity, and that intelligence is
in all that exists. The Supreme Being, although
possessing the highest power, is yet not without
bounds. He has been able to create the world only
in the conditions in which it is existing. In the
physical world, for instance, how could God have
made a body constituted like that of man and of the
animals indissoluble, or have made dissolution pain-
less? As for the moral world, how could he have
formed a being living and acting without love or
the passions that so often and so fatally lead him
astray? Yet these very imperfections and evils with
which our earth is afflicted attest that the supreme
intelligence has limits. God has wished to prevent
evil and failed, according to the tenet of Epicurus.

"Those who cry, All is well!" says Voltaire, in
his poem on Lisbon, "are charlatans. Evil exists, it
is absurd to deny it. The earth is but a vast field of
carnage and destruction. The individual man is a
very miserable being who has a few hours of rest, a
few moments of satisfaction, but a long series of
sorrowful days in his brief existence."

And in his *Candide*, his hero, after having gone
through a thousand unpleasant trials, after having
been a witness to the carnage of war, massacres, pes-
tilences, and earthquakes, exclaims,

"If this is the best of worlds, what must be the
others!"

Voltaire does not believe that the creator of the world governs it. But, through his utilitarianism and social bias, he admits him as a judge and remunerator:

"Is it more advantageous for the general good of such thinking and miserable beings as we are," he has written, "to recognize a God who rewards and punishes, who upholds and consoles us, or must we reject this idea and give ourselves up to our misery without a consolation and without a curb for our vices?"

"All nature," he wrote to the royal prince of ——, "has proved the existence of the supreme God to you; it remains for your heart to feel the existence of a just God. How could you be just if God were not? And how could he be just if he could neither reward nor punish?"

And in his treatise on *God and Men :*

"No society can exist without justice; let us therefore announce a just God. If the law of the State punishes known crimes, let us announce a God who will punish undetected crimes. Let a philosopher be a Spinozist if he will, but let the Statesman be a theist. You do not know who or what God is, how he punishes or rewards, but you know he must be sovereign reason, sovereign equity; that is enough. No mortal has a right to contradict you, since you state a thing probable and necessary to mankind."

Thoroughly conscious of the weak points and contradictions of his theodicy, Voltaire, like a true son of the eighteenth century, takes refuge in doubt, since certainty fails him:

"For my part, I am sure of nothing; I believe

there is an intelligent being, a creative power, a God.
I creep about in darkness about all the rest. I affirm
a belief to-day, doubt it to-morrow, and deny it the
next day; and each day I may have been mistaken.
All honest philosophers have acknowledged to me,
when they have had a drop of wine in them, that
the great Being has not given them a better share of
evidence than he has given me."

In his *Memoirs* he says again:

"The fact is that we know nothing of ourselves;
we have motion, life, sentiment, and thought without knowing how ; we are only blind creatures
walking about in the dark and reasoning in a groping
way" .

And elsewhere:

"Metaphysics have been, up to Locke, a vast field
of error.   Locke has really been useful only because
he has narrowed down the area wherein philosophy
aimlessly wandered.

"When we have discussed mind and matter, we
end by not understanding each other. No philosopher has ever been able to raise, by his own
strength, the veil nature has spread over the first
principles of things.

"I do not know the *quomodo*, it is true. I had
rather stop than go astray. Philosophy consists in
stopping when the torch of science fails us. I ob-
serve the phenomena of nature, but I admit I do not
understand first principles any better than you."

That was certainly good faith and frankness in a
philosopher !

It is still with the expression of doubts on first
causes that Voltaire ends his poem on the disaster of
Lisbon:

"What can of our poor mind the most extended flight?
Ah, naught! The book of fate is closed to our sight;
And man, to himself strange, to man remains unknown.
What am I? where am I? and wherefrom have I come?
Poor atoms tormented upon this muddy heap,
Whom death soon hurries off, whose fate is most to weep,
Yet *thinking* atoms, we, of whom the searching eyes
By thought uplift and led, have measured e'en the skies;
Into the infinite we plunge with eager wing,
Yet scarcely of ourselves can find or know a thing.
This earth where only reigns dark error, lust, and pride,
Is full of those who think all good in life doth bide;
Yet all complain, all grieve. E'er seeking joy or gain,
Man ne'er would die and still ne'er would be born again.
We sometimes, in the midst of all our woes and fears,
The hand of pleasure seek to brush away our tears;
But pleasure takes to wing, and like a phantom flees,
Whilst losses, pains, regrets are brought on every breeze.
The past does offer us but memories void of pith,
The present is a farce if the future be a myth,
If the drear hand of death the thinking soul destroys.
One day all shall be well, this is our hope, in sooth;
But, *all is well to-day*, nay, *that* is *not* the truth."

Voltaire, who separated God and nature, was not
a dualist with regard to the body and soul. They
are but one for him. What is understood by spirit
or soul is after all nothing more than mind, than
the faculty of thinking given to the refined matter of
the brain. He approaches Locke's definition, that it
is not impossible that God may have communicated
the faculty of thinking to a particle of matter, the
human brain. But he denies the immortality of the
soul, that is the survival of thought to the brain.
Man, he says, is like a musical instrument which gives
forth no sound after it is broken. Animals, like ourselves, have sensations, ideas, memory, desires, mo-

tives, and yet no serious thinker has ventured to attribute immortality to them. Why should we need such a thing to explain the little superiority in faculties and activity of thought of which, however, we are so proud? A divine power reveals itself in the sensations of the least of insects as in the brain of a Newton. But these sensations are themselves but a higher grade of effects from the same mechanical laws, which, emanating from God, act throughout all parts of nature. Some say they cannot conceive how sensation and thought may be imparted to extended or material being; but have we any ideas, asks Voltaire, concerning a being not extended? Matter and spirit are only words. We have no clearer conception of the one than the other. That is the reason why we cannot decide *à priori* as to what the one or the other is capable of. To deny to the body the faculty of thinking is no less bold than it would be to refuse it to the soul. But now, what is the soul? A being made up of faculties, as memory, will, speech, etc. Such beings have no existence. It is after all the *man* who wills, remembers, speaks. The soul, which we look upon as a being *per se*, is in reality nothing but a faculty granted to superior beings. "It is a faculty which has been mistaken for a substance."

In his *Treatise on Metaphysics*, written for Mme. du Châtelet, Voltaire declares that "his reason has taught him that all our ideas come to us through the senses;" he admits he cannot forbear laughing when he is told that men will still have ideas when they no longer have senses; he would as soon believe we shall eat and drink after death, when we have no longer any stomachs or mouths. "What! I refuse immortality to whatever animates that parrot, this thrush, this

dog, and I grant it to man simply because he desires
it? It would be very pleasant indeed to survive this
life eternally to preserve the most excellent part of our
being after the destruction of the other, to live forever surrounded with our friends, etc. This illusion
would be consoling amidst real sufferings. I do not
affirm I have positive demonstrations against the
spirituality and immortality of the soul, but all the
probabilities are against it."

As for the persecution of the good and the impunity
of the wicked, consequences of thus ranking the immortal soul among the chimeræ, Voltaire solved the
question simply by draping himself in the mantle of
the Stoicist. The virtuous man is rewarded by the
sentiment of having done his duty, by peace of
heart, by the friendship of the good. "It is Cicero's
opinion; it is that of Cato, of Marcus Aurelius, of
Epictetus; it is my own." "The wicked are punished
by remorse, which never fails, and by human justice,
which fails but rarely."

Firm in his deism while denying the immortality
of the soul, Voltaire asserts the freedom of the will
and comes forward as the champion of human liberty. To will and to act without being constrained,
that is to be free. Such is the freedom of the divine
nature, such is the freedom of man. The erroneous
opinion that man is not free comes from beholding
the passions which often against his will impel him
to certain acts; thus anger, love, pride. But to say
that man is not free because sometimes he is not, is to
say, Men are sick sometimes, therefore they are never
well. It is very certain that men are not all equally
free, as they are not all in equally sound health.

In common with Locke, Voltaire rejected innate

ideas. However, he admits we are not always masters of the ideas which enter our brain, and as this
avowal somewhat damages his free will doctrines, he
says that if ever our will is determined by our ideas,
moral perceptions must be counted among these.
"The idea of justice is so entirely recognized that
the greatest crimes which afflict human society are
all committed under a false appearance of justice.
The greatest, at least the most destructive, of these
crimes is war. But there is no aggressor who does
not deck his misdeed with the pretext of justice."

After sketching Voltaire's theodicy, it remains
for us to consider his struggle against Christianity,
of which he was the most formidable adversary.
He looks upon it as a series of impostures imposed
by audacious charlatans upon human credulity, as the
scourge of humanity, as a shroud thrown upon
thought and civilization throughout long centuries
of mourning, suffering and ignorance, and a tyrant
which for ages has crushed and debased the race by
its loathsome domination.

Voltaire began to express his opinions upon the
Christian doctrines in his famous *Ode to Urania,*
then in his *Philosophical Dictionary*, in his *Dinner
With the Count of Boulainvilliers*, and *passim*
throughout all his works.

Voltaire spares the personality of Jesus and dis-
tinguishes it from the idolatrous worship which has
been founded upon the apocryphal gospels. According to him, Jesus was never a Christian, *a fortiori,* a
Catholic. He would have repudiated such doctrines
with horror. "He was a sort of rustic Socrates, an
obscure man born among the dregs of the people.
who gave himself out as a prophet. as so many others

have done. He has written nothing, because he could not write, and he has founded a sect upon the enthusiasm of weak imaginations, just like the quaker, Fox, who preached his doctrine and traveled through the country dressed in leather."

Very different from our times, in which science refuses any place for miracles, either in nature or history, antiquity believed in prodigies, supernatural effects, and that especially among the Jews, a barbarous, ferocious, repulsive, and self-infatuated people. Jesus, having attacked the priests of his time, was crucified, and to avenge him his disciples corroborated the miraculous stories about him, especially that of his resurrection. In reality we know nothing of Jesus. On the worship of this individual has been based a religion which has caused more blood to flow than all "the most cruel wars." Jesus became the pretext of our fantastic doctrines and of our religious persecutions, but he was not their author.

When he discusses the foundations of the Christian religion, Voltaire sees in them nothing "but a mass of the flatest impostures invented by the vilest rabble, which alone embraced Christianity during the first hundred years. The Christians make up an uninterrupted series of counterfeiters. They forge letters of Jesus Christ, of Pilate, of Seneca; infamous archives of falsehood which have been called *pious frauds.*

What proves the falsity of the gospels, is their contradictory system of morals, good in what it extracts from the ancient philosophers, revolting in several of its tenets, breathing war and fanaticism, inspiring hatred against the family, against society, making itself the apologist of ignorance, foolishness, and idleness.

"Platonism is the father of Christianism of which the Jewish religion is the mother."

After riddling with his crushing irony the Bible, the Old and New Testaments, Voltaire wonders how mankind have ever been able to accept such idle stories and extravaganzas, born of uncultivated and coarse minds. The history of the whole Church is a mass of prodigious and absurd inventions; with punctilious and hair-splitting councils; its monarchism destructive of all society; its bishops and its popes inconceivably outrageous impostors and felons. "If it be evident that the life of the Church is a continuous series of quarrels, impostures, vexations, swindles, robberies, and murders, it is demonstrated then that the abuse is in the thing, in the system itself, just as it is plain that a wolf has always been ravenous."

Voltaire absolutely lacks in respect for the holy mass:

"Your Roman Catholics have carried their Catholic extravagance far enough to say that they change a piece of dough into a god, through the virtue of a few words in Latin, and that all the particles of that dough become so many gods and creators of the universe. A vagrant who has been consecrated a priest, a monk just out of the arms of a prostitute, will, for twelve sous, come all rigged up in a clownish dress, and mumble to me in a foreign tongue what you call a *mass*, split the air into four with his three fingers, bow, straighten up again, turn to the right and to the left, backward and forward, and make as many gods as suit him, drink them, eat them, and evacuate them afterward ! And you will not admit that it is the most monstrous and ridiculous idolatry which has ever dishonored human nature? Must not a man himself be changed into a dumb brute before he will imagine that white bread and red wine can be changed into a god ? Modern idolators, do not compare yourselves to the ancient who worshiped Zeus, the demiourgos, master of God and men, and did homage to secondary gods. Know that Ceres, Pomona, and Flora were far above your Ursula with her eleven thousand virgins, and that it does not beseem the priests of Mary Magdalene to laugh at the priests of Minerva."

At the end of the article on *Tolerance* in the *Philosophical Dictionary* Voltaire thus rails at the Bible and the Jews:

"I shall say to my brother the Chinaman, let us sup together without ceremony, for I do not like mummeries, but I like thy law, the wisest of all, and perhaps the most aged. I shall say pretty much the same thing to my brother the Hindoo. But what shall I say to my brother the Jew? Shall I give him to sup? Yes, provided that during the meal Balaam's ass does not take it into his head to bray, that Ezekiel does not attempt to mix his breakfast with our supper, that no fish will come and swallow some of our guests and keep them three days in its belly; that no serpent will come and mingle in the conversation to seduce my wife; that no prophet will presume to go to bed with her after supper, as did the good man Hosea for fifteen francs and a bushel of barley; and especially provided that no Jew will march around my house blowing his trumpet, tumble my walls to the ground, and slaugh-

ter me, my father, my mother, my wife, my children,
my cat, and my dog, according to the ancient Jewish
custom. Come, friends, let us have peace; let us all
say our *benedicite!*"

As for the social influences of the Christian religion, they have been most detrimental and disastrous.
Christianity has been a step backward, a retrogra-
dation, a return of mankind to primitive barbarism.
No religion has accumulated so many ruins or caused
such overwhelming darkness. The tolerating spirit
of the religions of pagan antiquity is well known.

Enumerating the murders, the massacres perpe-
trated during the fifteen centuries of the Christian
domination, Voltaire sets them at nine million four
hundred and eight thousand eight hundred men who
have perished by the hand or through the means of
Christianity. The Christians having grounded their
power on pious frauds and impostures, the rogues
became cruel and sanguinary toward those who ventured to doubt the legitimacy of their power or dared
to offer them the slightest opposition.

" From the Nicean Council to the sedition in the
Cevennes, there has not elapsed a single year in
which Christianity did not shed blood. Read only
the *Histoire Ecclésiastique!* See the Donatists and
their adversaries pelting one another; the Athana-
sians and Arians filling the Roman empire with
carnage for the sake of a diphthong! Hear those
barbarous Christians complaining that the wise
Emperor Julian forbids them to throttle and destroy
each other! Look at the frightful series of massacres: so many citizens dying on the scaffold, so many
princes assassinated; the fagots set ablaze by the
councils; twelve millions of innocent victims, inhab-

itants of a new hemisphere, slaughtered like wild
beasts in the hunt, under pretext that they will not
be Christians! And in our old hemisphere, behold
the Christians ceaselessly murdering each other;
aged men, children, mothers, wives, daughters,
expiring in crowds in the crusade against the Albigenses, against the Huguenots, the Calvinists, the
Anabaptists! Think of our St. Bartholomew, the
massacres in Ireland, in Piedmont, in the Cevennes,
whilst a bishop of Rome, lazily reclining on a bed of
repose, has his feet kissed, and fifty eunuchs exercise
in quavers and trills to divert him!"

In his *Philosophical Dictionnary*, after reckon-
ing up these religious murders, which he estimates
at nine and a half millions of people, either
slaughtered, drowned, burned, broken on the wheel,
or hung *for the love of God*, Voltaire adds this
stirring conclusion:

"Whoever thou mayest be, reader, if thou hast
preserved thy family archives, consult them, and
thou wilt see thou hast had more than one ancestor
immolated under the pretense of religion, or at least
cruelly persecuted (unless he was persecutor, which
must be still more melancholy). Whether thy name be
Argyle, Perth, Montrose, Hamilton, or Douglas, remember thy forefathers had their hearts torn out on a
scaffold because of a liturgy or of two yards of linen.
Art thou Irish? Then read the declaration of Parliament of the 25th of July, 1643. It says that in
the conjuration of Ireland there perished 154,000
Protestants by the hands of the Catholics. Believe,
with the advocate Brook, if thou wilt, that only
forty thousand defenseless men were slaughtered in
that holy and Catholic conspiracy. But whatever

thy choice may be, thou art a descendant of the
murderers or of the murdered. Choose and tremble!
But, O prelate of my native land, be thou joyful;
our blood has secured thee an income of a hundred
thousand guineas."

Voltaire was scarcely more favorably disposed
toward Protestantism. Protestant fanaticism is no
better than Catholic fanaticism. "The Reformation
itself," he says, "kindled the fire of persecution and
religious wars in Europe." He execrated Calvin because of Servetus's execution. If the Protestants
abolished the celibacy of priests, they threw open
the doors of the convents. Voltaire attacked the
Jansenists as well as the Jesuits. When the latter
were expelled from France he said the *foxes* had
truly been driven away, but only to leave room for
the *wolves* to feed upon the trembling philosophers.

Voltaire pays but little attention to the political
question. He remained, however, a monarchist and an
aristocrat. Republican Switzerland, where his books,
like those of Rousseau, were burnt, was not calculated to inpire him with love for the democratic form
of government. To him republican was a word of
very vague and empty signification, which he believed, moreover, somewhat synonymous with pro-
scription, intolerance, and mediocrity. He mistrust-
ed the masses and their use of power; he had seen
the republics of antiquity too often ostracize the
good and the illustrious. Voltaire was a partisan of
progress from the upper stratum, through the directing classes, as would be said to-day. He would
have acquiesced in the aristocratic doctrine of Saint
Simon, giving the reins of government to the most

capable and enlightened. He admired the English Constitution, with its royalty tamed and trained to the function of clerk of the nation.

"The English nation," he wrote, in his *Letters on the English*, "is the only one which ever succeeded in regulating the power of kings by resisting it, and which, through untiring efforts, has ever succeeded in establishing that wise government in which the prince, all-powerful to do good, is bound hand and foot and powerless to do evil; in which the nobles are great without insolence and without vassals, whilst the people share in the administration of affairs without confusion. The government of England is not intended for great brilliancy. Its aim is not the splendid folly of making conquests, but is rather to prevent its neighbors from making any. This nation is not simply watchful of its own liberty; it is also careful of the liberty of others. It has certainly cost dearly to establish liberty in England, the idol of despotic power has been drowned in seas of blood, but the English do not think they have bought their system of law at too high a price. Other nations have not had any less trouble, have not spilled any less blood than they, but the blood which they spilled in the cause of liberty has only served to cement their servitude."

And in another passage of his *Letters*, which refers to the English ecclesiastics, he says:

"When they know that in France young men known for their debauchery, and raised to the priesthood through the influence of women, publicly give themselves up to love, amuse themselves with composing tender couplets, give every day protracted and dainty suppers, and from these occupations go

and invoke the Holy Ghost, and boldly style themselves successors to the apostles, they thank God for
being Protestants. Yet they are themselves but a
lot of ugly heretics worthy to be burned 'to all the
devils,' as François Rabelais puts it. That is why
I do not meddle with their affairs."

Thus Voltaire is seen to be an admirer of British
institutions and English limited royalty. But his
monarchic ideal, his typical king, implied the qualities of the philosopher. Sovereigns should be the
agents of progress, enlightened protectors of the sciences, letters, and art. This is what inspired him
with such an admiration for Louis XIV. He had
drawn up and defended this programme before the
king of Prussia while opposing his bellicose ten-
dency and exhorting him to be a truly philosophical
king—an Antoninus. But Frederick added the love
of conquest to his philosophy, and by way of pastime
conquered Silesia !

In his views of political economy Voltaire was
vacillating. In his *Man with the Forty Crowns* he
had first railed at the physiocrats, but later his views
identified themselves with the doctrines of De Quesnay.

Liberty and justice were the culminating points of
Voltaire's reformatory aspirations, and his incessant
preoccupation. Liberty, as he views it, consists in
defending only on equitable laws. Justice is to be
administered by upright judges, inaccessible to any

---

*François Quesnay, born in 1695, an eminent French econ-
omist and advocate of free trade, who had for followers Turgot,
Mirabeau, and others. He is the inventor of the term Political
Economy.

other sentiment than that of right. We have already seen what struggles he had carried on against the parliaments in order to drag their victims away from them, and with what persistency he clamored for the revising of the codes and for judiciary reforms. In all the voluminous writings of Voltaire we meet with the affirmation of the doctrines of liberty, emancipation of the mind, and inalienability of the rights of man. In the face of the censure of that detestable legislation which burnt all polemical productions on the subjects of politics or religion, and sentenced their authors to death or banishment, he wrote:

"The right to say and to print what we think is the right of every free man, a right of which he can not be deprived except through the exercise of the most odious tyranny. . . Sustaining the liberty of the press is the foundation of all other liberties; it is through it we mutually enlighten one another.

"The nations which have been the most enslaved have always been the ones that were most deprived of knowledge.

"The more my countrymen seek after truth, the more will they love their liberty.

"The same strength of mind that leads us to the true makes good citizens of us. What is it, in fact, to be free? It is to reason correctly; it is to know the rights of man; and when we know them well, we defend them likewise.

"It has never been attempted to impose the belief of foolish things upon men except for the purpose of subduing them.

"The more we become reasonable beings, the more we shall be free.

"I recommend to you," he also wrote, "truth, lib-

erty, and virtue, the three objects for which alone
we should care to live."

Voltaire thinks that as human beings we are all
equal, but not as members of society. The best constitution, he says, is that by which all trades, occupations, and professions are equally protected by the
law. Among the different classes, he evinced special interest in the peasant class, and sharply fought
against the oppressions that weighed upon them. He
delivered the peasant serfs from the mortmain and
the canons of Saint Claude. In his *Request to All
the Magistrates of the Kingdom* he said on this
point:

"Every man has an individual right of free disposition as to his person, property, and family. Legislation is the art of happiness and security for the
people; laws in opposition to this stand in contra-
diction with their very object; they should be given
up."

Voltaire vigorously denounced convents as a source
of ruin and sterility in the countries where they became established. He constantly opposed the privileges of the clergy, especially its exemption from
taxes and other burdens incumbent on all citizens.

In a word, there is not an abuse, not an error, prejudice, or infraction against the law of justice and
humanity, which has not been attacked or redressed
by Voltaire during his tempestuous life.

His valiant and glorious career sums up the history of progress in the eighteenth century to the
Revolution of '89, which crowned his philosophical
work.

THE ENEMIES OF
VOLTAIRE.

XXII. —THE ENEMIES OF VOLTAIRE.

Libels have accumulated against Voltaire. There is not a Catholic viper that has not worn out its fangs upon the Voltarian file.

To Travenol and Mannory has been attributed a voluminous collection of libels upon Voltaire, published in 1748, and entitled *Voltairiana*. This, according to Guerard, contains a multitude of inaccuracies and assumptions without foundation of fact.

Voltairiana has been plagiarized or reproduced in part by the anti-Voltairian libelists Harel, the abbé Baruel, the abbé Chaudon, Deluc, the Count of Allonville, the abbé Martin, Paillet de Warcy, Berchoux, Lepan, and a pack of other abbés and Jesuits. The attack of Lepan was published in 1817. From all the facts he reports, disfigured and distorted, he concludes:

That Arouet Voltaire was, 1. A bad son; 2. A bad citizen; 3. A false friend; 4. Envious; 5. A flatterer; 6. Ungrateful; 7. A calumniator; 8. Selfish; 9. An Intriguer; 10. With little delicacy; 11. Vindictive; 12. Eager for offices, honors, and dignities; 13. A hypocrite; 14. A miser; 15. Intolerant; 16. Wicked; 17. Inhuman; 18. Despotic; 19. Violent.

It may be said that Lepan's conclusions are worthy of his premises.

All these rabid Catholics, after having spit out their venom upon the character of Voltaire, seek above all to dishonor his last moments by their mon-

strous and false inventions. . The complete refutation
of these clerical impostures is found in the *Mémoires*
of Wagnières, Voltaire's amanuensis.

Not the least violent among these enemies of Voltaire was the count Joseph de Maistre.*

"The great crime of Voltaire," he wrote, "was the
abuse of talent and the deliberate prostitution of a
genius created to praise God and virtue. Not one
trait to redeem him; his corruption is of a kind that
belongs only to himself. It takes root in the deep-
est fibers of his heart, and takes ever-renewing and
increasing strength from all the powers of his understanding.

"Ever allied to sacrilege, it defies God and ruins
men. With a fury without an example, this insolent
blasphemer goes to the extent of declaring himself
the personal enemy of the Savior of men; he dares
from the depths of his nothingness to give him a
ridiculous name; and that adorable law which the
man-god brought upon earth, he calls the *infamous*.
Abandoned of God, who punishes by withdrawing
his presence, he henceforth knows no curb. Other
cynics astonished virtue; Voltaire astonishes vice
itself. He wallows in the mire and feeds upon it;
he gives his imagination up to *the enthusiasm of hell,*
which lends him all its strength to drag him on to
the bounds of evil. He invents prodigies, monsters
that appal us. Paris crowned, Sodom would have
banished him.

"How shall I describe what he makes me feel?
When I see what he could have done and what he
did, his inimitable talents inspire me only with a

---

*Joseph de Maistre, an eminent legitimist writer, 1753–1821.

kind of nameless, holy rage. . . Halting between admiration and horror, I would sometime have a statue raised to him . . by the hand of the executioner!"

After this incoherent reproof from the Count de Maistre, M. Ernest Hello seems very tame and insipid in his brochure, published in 1858, under the title of *M. Renan; Germany and Atheism in the Nineteenth Century.*

"Voltaire's attitude toward Christianity," he says, "is a frank one. It is complete blindness. It is a tranquillity born of absolute stupidity. Unable to conceive anything, he avoids even the trouble of seeking after it. Besides, his heart fitly seconds his mind. Voltaire, to define him cursorily, is an *unclean imbecile.*"

M. Louis Veuillot could not fail to give, in the Attic style we know so well, the final donkey's kick to our philosopher. According to this sexton of the Catholic press, "Voltaire was in his person a precious rascal. *All are agreed on this point.* His apologists attest, not voluntarily, indeed, but, unanimously, his infamy. (?) Impossible to admire him, to quote him, without proving at once that this great man possessed all the elements of a frightful scamp; . . . he mocks at everything, lies, betrays, hates, has no country, no honor, no God, no family. He is Satan himself, not crushed and annihilated, but victorious, placidly victorious."

After having exhausted his repertory of billingsgate, M. Veuillot finds it very pleasant and just that Voltaire should have been "embastilled, exiled, and caned."

But how he could return the blow, this detested

Voltaire, and how fortunate you are, Master Veuillot, not to have lived in the time of your worthy ancestors, Fréron, Desfontaines, Nonotte and Patouillet!

M. Nicolardot, in a bulky volume published in 1854, and entitled, *Household and Finances of Voltaire,* accuses him of shameless speculations. A few words of explanation are necessary.

Voltaire scarcely drew any profit for his numerous publications, and on this head he could not be stigmatized with the words of Proudhon, "*Writer is equivalent to swindler.*" He gave the most of his works gratuitously to his editors. Had he depended solely upon his revenue as an author, he would have lived in great poverty. But he said with truth that a man of letters must not be poor, for poverty hinders and shackles thought.

Voltaire became rich through some fortunate but very legitimate commercial speculations. Some time after his exile to England, he utilized the important sums he had received through the subscription to his *Henriade.* He speculated in the manufacture of paper by a new process, and also in the exportation of grain. Besides these happy ventures, he had the good fortune to win the capital prize in the Parisian lottery inaugurated by M. Pelletier des Forts. In Ferney we have seen this universal man become an agriculturalist, a manufacturer, a merchant. The only money transaction in which he erred was in connection with the Jew Hirsch in Prussia. This speculation consisted in forcing the sale of Saxon values payable to the Prussians. Some misunderstandings with the Jew were carried before the courts. Voltaire gained his case. It is none the less true that the speculation was not a laudable one. The king of Prussia reproached him with having compromised himself with a Jew, and Voltaire frankly acknowledged himself in the wrong. Apart from this slight error, what can Voltaire be accused of except of having, through his activity and intelligent enterprise, acquired a fortune which made him master of his thought?

The abbé Maynard (*Voltaire, his Life and Works,* 1847) finds that " Voltaire was a great comedian, and the only good comedy of which he was the author was that of his life, with its numberless and ever-varying scenes."

Among other crimes, he charges him with having calumniated the Jesuits ! and ends by apostrophizing him as a *Pulcinello,* insolvent debtor, veritable jail-bird, old histrion, etc.

Such are in brief all the varieties of calumny, all the Catholic arguments, invectives, and filth laid by the abbés, Jesuits, and holy water pamphleteers at the foot of Voltaire's statue.

Although he may strictly be numbered among Voltaire's enemies, we must not confound M. Renan with the mob of anti-Voltairian scribblers. He has never failed in a true writer's dignity while opposing in Voltaire the adversary of the Christian legend of which he has made a specialty. His most severe criticism bears on the alleged fact that Voltaire had ignored antiquity, by which is probably meant Hebraic and Christian antiquity. Notwithstanding, the author of the *Philosophical Dictionary,* although not acquainted with Hebrew, was not less learned even on these topics than the author of the *Life of Jesus.* So do his works prove him to have been.

Voltaire has been attacked and abused in verse as well as in prose. We insert a few of the epigrams of which he was the object.

Epigram from Piron :

> I saw to-day in Pigal's store
> A model I had heard much spoken of before.
> I saw the crushing eye, the glance with evil flame,
> The air of deep chagrin at thought of others' fame,
> And cried, "Ah, tell me not that here I see Voltaire :
> A monster 'tis!"   "Oh," said a certain pamphleteer,
>   "If 'tis a monster, that's the name !"

Another, attributed to J. J. Rousseau :

> With less of genius than of wit,
> Without faith, virtue, honor, grit,
> As he had lived he died the same,
> Bedecked with glory and with shame.

Another, by Dr. Young, on the occasion of the criticism upon the *Paradise Lost,* of Milton :

> Thy wit, thy homely face, thy form so lank and thin,
> Reveal thee now as death, as devil, and as sin.

Another, on the occasion of the dedication of *Mohammed* to Benoit XIV.:

> Dost know the purpose of a gift
> The pope has made to our Voltaire ?
> "Oh," comes the answer, rough and swift,
> "That mystery I can lay bare.
> The pope to the old dog has merely thrown a bone,
> As once to Aretino* they did in times agone."

---

* Pietro Aretino, an Italian author and wit of the sixteenth century, who, in spite of a sometimes too free pen, obtained the patronage of the pope.

VOLTAIRE AS A POET AND TRAGIC AUTHOR.

XXIII.—VOLTAIRE AS A POET AND TRAGIC AUTHOR.

Voltaire has left us twenty-eight tragedies and fifteen comedies or operas.

Nanine excepted, his comedies do not rise above mediocrity. He does not possess the *vis comica*.

In his tragedies he remained entirely within the classical limits, preserving the three unities of action, time, and place, and discarding as contrary to decorum the realism and theatrical outbursts of Shakspere. In 1732, the time his *Zaïre* was being played, he criticised the English theater as follows:

" You [English] must submit to the rules of our theater just as we must adopt your philosophy. We have made as good experiments on the human heart as you have done in physics. The art of pleasing seems to be the Frenchman's art; that of thinking seems to be yours."

Voltaire was mistaken in his estimate of the English theater. Since the sixteenth century, with their immortal Shakspere at their head, the English had been the masters of the stage. Classical tragedy, with its court costume and trappings, sacrificing the true to the conventional, the ease and strength of nature to the stiffness of etiquette, was inferior to the Shaksperian drama.

The brilliancy and superiority of Voltaire's tragedies consist in the fine and frequent strokes of wit that immediately passed as so much current money from hand to hand, and the powerful ideas that were repeated everywhere and became at once the philosophical maxims of the age. His theatrical writings were simply a continuation of the polemics of his books. But these pleadings, beautiful as they were, injured the action—destroyed, in part, the reality of the characters and situations. For this reason he must stand second to Shakspere and Corneille as a dramatic author, although he remains the foremost of his age as a tragic writer and poet.

In epic poetry, Voltaire eliminated the marvelous and in its stead substituted allegory—"a perceptible truth," as he terms it in his *Essay on Poetry*. Until he came, the marvelous, the divine, had been the soul, the life of the epic. These allegories and philosophical tirades, taking the place of lyric enthusiasm, have the fault, however, of imparting to the pages of the *Henriade* a certain coldness, a dryness, a lack of emotion. But the author sustains himself by his great ideas, his easy versification, his sparkling wit, as also by the happy choice of a sympathetic subject, since he celebrates Henry IV., the king who established peace and tolerance after a lengthy religious war rich in the atrocities of fanatical rage and hatred. Our readers already know the *Henriade* was published in London after some fruitless endeavors on the part of Voltaire to have it appear in France.

"I praise the spirit of peace and religious tolerance too much in that poem," he says; "I tell too many truths to the see of Rome. I throw too little venom at the Protestants to hope they would permit me to

publish in my native land a poem written in honor
of the greatest king it ever had."

It may be of interest to our readers to introduce
here a few quotations from the *Henriade*. The first
canto begins as follows:

> That hero, I now sing, who once reigned over France
> By double right of sword and just inheritance;
> To whom misfortunes taught to govern and to thrive ;
> Who could the factions soothe, or vanquish and forgive;
> Who foiled Mayenne, the Ligue, the hated foreigner,
> Who was a father to the land, as well as conqueror."

In the course of his second canto, Voltaire depicts
in burning words the horrible and murderous night
of the St. Bartholomew. It is a Huguenot who
speaks:

> " Who could the outrages succeed e'er to express,
> Of which that fatal night received the black impress?
> The death of Coligny, the murderers' highest mark,
> Of all their fury still was but a feeble spark.
> A maddened rabble now in ruthless, lawless bands
> All Paris overspread, and wearing in their hands
> A guilty steel, while flashed their hatred in their eyes,
> Upon our bleeding brethren trod with wild, triumphant cries.
> At their head Guise was seen, who, boiling o'er with ire,
> Avenged upon our friends the shade of his dread sire.
> Nevers, Gondi, Tavenne, with the assassin's steel,
> Incensed the cruel fire of their inhuman zeal,
> And with the list they'd drawn to serve or greed or hate,
> They led the throng and marked each victim for its fate.

> I shall not paint to you the tumult and the screams ;
> The blood on every side outpoured in gory streams ;
> The son upon the sire, by ruthless demons slain,
> And brother with sister, and maid with mother, lain ;
> The bride and groom struck down beneath their burning
>   roof ;

The babes dashed on the stones. But hold, I've said enough !
Such deeds of human rage, alas, we may conceive,
But what posterity will haply ne'er believe,
And which you scarcely now from my lips dare to trust.
These men, now mad with rage and filled with murd'rous
    thirst,
Excited by the voice of their blood-reeking priests,
Invoked the Lord and slew their fellow-men like beasts.
And with their hands thus soiled with that most guiltless
    blood,
The frightful incense dared to offer up to God."

The comic poem of the *Maid* (Joan of Arc, the Maid of Orleans), which gave so much trouble to Voltaire, shocks our modern ideas. The eccentric element in a peasant girl, living with the soldiery and fighting under a soldier's garb, is completely hidden from us by her patriotic devotion and enthusiasm. But the taste of to-day is not that of the preceding age. The favor with which the production met is characteristic of the period. The press could not supply copies of the *Pucelle* rapidly enough for the demand, and its most devoted readers were the great ladies of the court. But notwithstanding his licentious pleasantries, for which we can only blame him, the author respects the patriotic sentiment in the peasant girl of Domremy,* condemned and led to the stake by a bishop and an inquisitor.

Voltaire shines equally at the two poles of the poetical sphere; superior as he is in the philosophical poem, he shows inimitable grace and wit in his tales in verse, his light and fugitive pieces, and his odes, whilst his epigrams abound in arch puns and sharp,

---

* Domremy, her birthplace, a village in the Department of Vosges, northeastern France.

telling hits. We shall now reproduce several of these smaller pieces, beginning with an ode to Madame de Rupelmonde, written in 1722:

THE FOR AND AGAINST.

'Tis then thy will, fair Uranie,
That now, at thy behest, a new Lucretius born,
    By my undaunted hand, for thee
The veil of superstition may be torn ;
That I expose to view the sad and dangerous sight
Of all the holy lies that fill the earth with blight,
    And that, through my philosophy,
The horrors of the tomb thou mayest learn to scorn,
And all the foolish dread of the life yet unborn.
Believe not that by lust or by mad error led,
    I stand before thee now to rail and to blaspheme,
Thus hoping to avert penalty from my head,
    If I but slay the law that rules o'er sin supreme.
But enter after me, with a respectful tread,
    Within the holy sanctuary
Of him to us announced, but to our view denied.
I would love God. I seek a friend in him. Ah, me !
A tyrant am I shown, who can inspire but dread,
His image did that God once stamp upon our face,
But the more to degrade and deeply curse our race,
    And deadly sin he made us like,
    To have the better right to strike ;
He tempted us with pleasures bright,
The more to torture us in the infernal night
With pains forever fed by his eternal might.
No sooner had that God upon our face impressed
    His image, when he did repent,
As if the maker shouldn't, as to the task he bent,
Its faults have noticed and suppressed.
In favors he is blind, in wrathful moods as blind,
And scarce had made when he would fain destroy mankind.
He bids the heaving sea the new-born earth to flood,
That earth which in six days from chaos he had brought.

Perhaps will he at last, now grown a wiser God
Create a world more pure in action, word, and thought ;
    Alas, no ! for the race he curst,
    He drags another from the dust,
A race of craven slaves and tyrants mad with lust,
    A race tenfold worse than the first.
What will his course be now ? what thunderbolts, what fires
Are now his mighty hands to hurl down from above ?
Hear now ! O Prodigy, O Mystery, O Love !
    That God who had just drowned the sires,
    To save the wicked sons expires.

There is an obscure race of low and fickle mind,
Whom superstitious lusts do repeatedly tempt,
The easy prey of all, the butt of humankind,
And ever doomed to feel the world's supreme contempt ;
And God, almighty God, forgetting his estate,
Is born a child among the race all men despise ;
A Jewess in her womb brings him to human state,
Around her feet he crawls, and has before her eyes
    All childhood's low infirmities.

For years an obscure wretch, with hammer in his hand,
He loses his best days in such unworthy toil ;
Last having preached three years around his native land,
    He dies while thieves scoff and revile.
At least the blood of God, for sinful mortals slain,
Was surely deemed a price sufficient to restrain
    The blows which vengeful Satan would
    Heap on our head, in hellish mood.
What ! God has willed to die to save all men from ruin,
And yet it is in vain he dies !
What ! shall his clemency be vaunted to the skies,
When he resumes his wrath against our cancelled sin,
And to the abyss again condemns us for all times.
When his dark rage foils all that for our sake he did,
And after having spilled his blood for all our crimes,
He crushes us for deeds that we did not commit !
This God doth visit still with unabated ire
Upon his last offspring the sins of their first sire ;

He calls for an account upon a thousand tribes,
Yet wrapped within their errors' night,
   And punishment in hell contrives
For the ignorance himself put on us as a blight,
Whilst we are told that he to save poor mortals strives!
   America, thou land so vast,
Ye nations born beside the gateways of the sun !
   Ye tribes on northern limits cast,
Whom error holds in sway, shall you, then, every one,
   Because you knew not that of yore,
In a strange hemisphere, in Syria or what not,
A workman's child upon a Jewish maid begot,
By Peter thrice denied, a shameful torture bore ?
I fail to recognize in these unworthy traits
   The holy one I would adore;
   I should dishonor God the more
By such belittling faith and such unsuited praise.

But listen now, O God, from thy ethereal throne,
   To my earnest and plaintive cry;
   Thou wilt not frown upon my incredulity,
My heart to thee is too well known.
The fool reviles thee, but the wise revere thy way;
No Christian I, but 'tis more truthfully to own,
To love thee and thy law—to worship and obey,

But what dread object now appears before my sight?
'Tis he! 'tis he, the Christ, in all his pomp and might!
Beside him, on a fleecy cloud,
The emblem of his death, the cross, is bathed in light.
Beneath his powerful feet lies Death wrapped in her shroud.
Against the gates of hell he's fought and won the fight,
His reign has been announced by prophets far around;
His throne cemented by the glorious martyrs' blood.
The ways of all his saints in miracles abound,
He's vouched them heavenly joys when in their last abode ;
As his example once, his moral is divine ;
He comforts in secret the faithful who repine ;
In all their woes he stands, aye ready to aid them;

And if on fraud, alas! his doctrine must recline,
Yet are we fortunate to be deceived by him.

Between these two portraits, inquiring Uranie,
For the uncertain truth, now seek with fullest scope,
Now gifted with a mind which, 'faith, alone could be
Full able with thy charms to cope.
Bethink thee the most high, in omniscience divine,
Has graven in thy heart, as he has done in mine,
    A natural religion there.
Believe it, were thy mind to err from bad to worse,
Ne'er could it be the aim of his eternal curse.

Be sure before his throne of any time or race
The just shall find a resting-place.
Believe the humble bonze or charitable heart
With him shall find more plenteous grace
Than Jansenist with soul so hard,
Or pope with false and haughty face.
Why should he care, indeed, by what name he's adored?
All homage is received, but none exalts the Lord.
Of all our zealous care what can a god have need?
We could offend him but with some inhuman deed.
    It is our goodness he esteems,
    And not our praise which precious seems.

THOU AND YOU.

ODE TO THE MARQUISE DE GOUVERNET.

O Phyllis, where is now the time
When in a cab we rode the town?
No footman, no adornments thine,
Thou hadst no charms beyond thine own.
With a bad supper, blithe and free,
Which thou for me ambrosial made,
Thou seem'dst to care for none but me,
Thy happy dupe, ah, fickle maid,
With all my life enwrapt in thee!
Thou possessed then nor wealth nor rank,
The fates alone hadst thou to thank

For loveliness wont with thy age;
A heart too tender to be sage;
A marble breast and beauteous eyes—
With charms like these a precious prize.
Alas! who roguish would not be?
And so thou wert, ah, wicked nymph;
And yet (Cupid forgive it me)
I loved thee but the more, thou imp!
Ah, Madam, now your stately life,
With honors every day so rife,
From those sweet moments, oh, how far!
That giant with white hair and scar,
Who guards your doors with lies so bland,
Of time the image, seems to mar
All sweets by chasing off the band
Of tender loves and playful smiles.
Beneath your roofs and gorgeous piles
These children tremble to appear.
Alas! I have seen them of yore
Thy window climb without a fear,
And play within thy humble door.
No, Madam, carpets on your floor,
Though wove by La Savonnerie,
Though brought away from Persian store,
And all your precious jewelry,
Those costly dishes which Germain
Engraved with art well-nigh divine,
And bowers where, though not with ease,
Martin surpasses the Chinese;
Your vases of Japan so white,
Yea, all these fragile, marvelous things,
Those diamond cascades so bright
Upon your ears, your costly rings;
Those pearly carcanets upon
Your neck, of yore so heavenly smooth,
With all your pomp, are not worth one
Of the sweet kisses of thy youth.

To this ode Phyllis, marchioness of Gouvernet, who
had been Suzanne de Livry, answered by a quatrain
borrowed from Voltaire:

> Let us now to·beautiful youth
> Leave its playful, wanton freedom;
> We live but two moments, forsooth,
> Let the last belong to wisdom.

THE *I HAVE SEEN.*

Here follow the principal passages of the *J'ai Vu*
of Louis Lebrun, published after the death of Louis
XIV. Attributed to Voltaire, *who was not twenty
years of age*, it occasioned his first embastillement.
But this was but the pretext for his incarceration.
In reality the regent had ordered it upon being informed by the spy Beauregard that a pamphlet in
Latin verse by Voltaire was being circulated, which
begun with these words, *Regnante puero*, and in
which the author energetically denounced the incests
and vices of Philippe of Orleans.

> Yes, I hav seen, distressful sight!
> I have seen La Bastille, Vincennes
> Le Chatelet besides a thousand more vile pens,
> With faithful subjects filled, the kingdom's stay and light.
>
> I have seen in a woman's gown
> A demon rule with smile or frown.
> Her God, her soul, her faith, she betrayed; anything
> To shape and lead the mind of her too credulous king.
> I have seen in those direful days
> The foe of all our race, of our beloved land,
> In Paris exercise with murderous sword in hand
> A tyranny most dark and base;
> Hypocrisy triumph, and virtuous men abhorred;
> I have seen, 'tis enough, the Jesuit adored.
> All this I saw in our great king's most baneful reign,

Whom God, to meet our prayer, saw fit to send of yore,
To punish us withal.   Yes, all this have I seen,
And yet my years in life will not count up a score.

STANZAS.

THE WRONGS.

No, 'tis not wrong to dare to say
What honest minds think and obey;
And bold, wise men do own the right
All things to speak, all things to write.

These forty years have I defied
Those who the mind have dwarfed and tied ;
To your small State*, by fate now led,
'Twere wrong to unsay what I have said.

The Evil One, too oft, I know,
Has hid his tail and furtive claw
Beneath a holy pope's attire
Or Calvin's cloak and saintly ire.

I do no wrong when I attest
The holy slayers I detest
Who sweep the earth with fire and sword
To serve a kind and loving Lord.

Yes, to the last I shall be proud
To have proclaimed my faith aloud ;
And I will dare to weep and sigh
O'er a Dubourg or a Servet.

The hellish folly could not last ;
The horrid frenzy now is past ;
Fanaticism is lying low,
But dark hypocrisy reigns now.

Buffoons with the ill-fitting cloak,
The saintly mien, the silly talk,

---

*Belgium.

The wretched music, and worse song,
  If I despise you, am I wrong?

EPIGRAMS AND MADRIGALS.

TO MADAME LA DUCHESSE DE LA VALLIERE,

WHEN SENDING HER A SHUTTLE.

The figure's plain to all our eyes—
  If Friendship, Love, and Graces three,
Can ever make a warp which even gods would prize,
  The shuttle must be thrown by thee.

INSCRIPTION ON A STATUE OF LOVE.

Whatever thy name, here thy master thou dost see,
For such he must be now, has been, or else shall be.

EPITAPH OF THE POPE CLEMENT XIII.

Here lies the haughty chief of Christians far and near,
  Of Bourbons e'er the sworn, the inveterate foe;
As vicar of the Christ, to us he did appear,
  But with his curate, sure, must be at variance now.

UPON A RELIQUARY.

Of superstition this, my friend,
  To folly is a gift most rare ;
The news to Reason do not send ;
  The holy Church we still must spare.

ON THE PROPHETS.

The gods to their interpreter
  Have made a marvelous gift indeed ;

For none can prophesy well ere
He first of reason is bereaved.

———

TO THE CHURCH BELL RINGERS.

(WRITTEN WHEN TEN YEARS OF AGE.)

Ye persecutors of the race
Who so relentlessly do ring
Your bells, and murder us apace,
Would God ye were choked with the string!

———

UPON THE STAMP

PLACED BY THE PUBLISHER, LEJOY, AT THE HEAD OF A COMMENTARY
UPON THE "HENRIADE," AND IN WHICH VOLTAIRE'S PORTRAIT
FIGURED BETWEEN THOSE OF LA BAUMELLE AND FRERON.

Lejoy has placed Voltaire between
Freron and LaBaumelle, they say.
It would make a true Calvary,
If a *good* thief were on the scene.

———

IMPROMPTU ON TURGOT.

I hold firm faith in thee, Turgot.
What thou wouldst do I do not know,
Nor care, since 'tis the contrary
Of what was done before thy day.

———

TO HELVETIUS.

Thy lines seem drawn indeed by fair Apollo's hand;
My gratitude shall be thy only recompense.
Thy book has been composed with Reason's magic wand;
Then haste and leave; away from France!

UPON LEFRANC DE POMPIGNAN,

BISHOP OF PUYS-EN-VELAY.

Do you ken why old Jeremiah
   In Judea wept his whole life long ?
It was he saw with prophet's eye
   He'd be translated by Le Franc.

ON THE BANKRUPTCY OF THE RECEIVER-GEN. ERAL MICHEL.

(HE HELD £32,500 OF VOLTAIRE'S MONEY.)

Once Michel, in the Eternal's name,
The devil put to flight and shame.
But after this, I can freely tell,
I hope the devil may singe him in h—l.

ON BOYER, BISHOP OF MIREPOIX,

WHO ASPIRED TO THE CARDINAL'S HAT.

In vain does fortune now prepare
To gift thee with her favors rare;
The more thy fate shall rise and beam,
The more a ninnie thou wilt seem.
The pope may well give thee a hat,
But brains! God only can do that.

TO THE KING OF PRUSSIA,

WHILE RETURNING HIM THE KEY OF CHAMBERLAIN AND THE CROSS OF HIS ORDER.

It was with joy they were received,
It is with grief they are released,
So lovers, made by aught irate,
Return the portrait of their mate.

In answer to some verses sent him by the Society
of Tolerance in Bordeaux:

> But how? You wish to build in France
> A temple to fair tolerance !
> Then at her sacred altars I
> Shall come to kneel, to pray, to sigh.
>
> Perchance some stones I may have dressed
> That will fit in well with the rest
> In your strong wall. With them, alack !
> I was almost stoned by the bigot pack.
>
> But well I know the gospel's law,
> And lowly bow to heavenly rules,
> So, as good Christians should, I now
> Forgive them all, both knaves and fools.

Voltaire did not write to the living alone; he also
addressed the illustrious dead. We could scarcely
close this volume more fitly than with the following
significant extract from his *Ode to Horace:*

> 'Fore thee, sweet Tiber, sketched by such a master's hand
> Of Epicurus, e'en the vaunted gardens pale.
> Yet Ferney does to me appear the fairest land.
> The charmed eye now rests on verdant hill and vale,
> Now views Geneva's sea reflecting the blue sky;
> Afar the rugged Alps uplift their crests on high,
> Yet lovingly embrace the valleys at their base,
> Which, scattered through the elms, luxuriant vineyards grace.
> And, from this shore, O bard, I whisper it to thee,
> On Tiber's bank, "Thrice happy is the people that is free."

UNPUBLISHED LETTERS OF VOLTAIRE AND MADAME DU CHATELET.

We have found in the *Archives* of Brussels a single manuscript letter of Voltaire and several of Madame du Chatelet, of which, however, we shall publish but one, since the others refer only indirectly to M. de Voltaire.

Voltaire's letter is dated on the 16th of June, 1742. It is addressed from Paris to Monsieur Charlier, *counselor to the sovereign council of Brabant, opposite the Dominicans, Brussels :*

" "I have heard of the loss you have experienced with great concern. The obligations under which you have put Madame du Châtelet can only add to the interest one must take in all that concerns you as soon as he has the honor of knowing you. I have hope soon to return to Brussels and renew the expression of the tender and respectful sentiments with which I shall remain all my life, Monsieur.

" Your humble and obedient servant,

" VOLTAIRE."

As may be seen from the above, Voltaire could wield a soft and caressing pen when he willed, as well as the acerb and penetrating quill he so effectively used against his enemies. Indeed, when we have honestly studied this great man, we are irresistibly drawn to the conclusion that his nature was intrinsically tender and affectionate; but injustice and hypocrisy roused within the depths of his heart those welling springs of hatred, gall, and satire which made him so redoubtable to all the foes of justice.

The letter of Madame du Châtelet is also dated from Paris, December 9, 1746, and addressed to the same person, M. Charlier, Brussels. She writes concerning her lawsuit with the house of Hoensbroeck:

"Dearest friend," she writes, "I hope now in none but you. Let me know what I can depend upon and what I should do, for I am in despair.

"This Friday, Dec. 9th."

And in the way of postscriptum we read on the *verso:*

"My son and M. de Voltaire send you a thousand compliments. It is positively true that the pope has sent him two beautiful gold medals whereon his portrait is engraved and has written him a charming letter. I will send you a copy, if you wish to see it in the original, or else a translation in French."

NOTES.

The titles of the works of Voltaire condemned to be burned by the Paris Parliament are:

The Philosophical Letters ; Natural Religion ; A Summary of Ecclesiastes and the Song of Solomon ; The Philosophical Dictionary ; God and Men ; The Testament of the Curé Meslier, (edited and published by Voltaire); *The Dinner with the Count of Boulainvilliers ; The Man with the Forty Crowns. A Collection of Pieces, The Voice of the People, The Diatribe against the Author of the Ephemerides,* were suppressed by the Council.

Besides, Voltaire was *interdicted* by twenty-five decrees of the see of Rome.

The dedication of *Ædipus to Madame* (1718) is signed Arouet de Voltaire.

The true origin of Voltaire's name is absolutely unknown. Some biographers have attributed it to some property owned by the philosopher, others to an anagram of the name Arouet l. j. (*le jeune*, the young or junior), by changing the *u* into *v* and the *j* into *i*. After all, the name, Voltaire, may have simply resulted from the fancy of the man who made it so illustrious.

At a reading of the *Henriade*, which took place during the year 1723 at the house of the president de Maisons, the poem being the object of numerous criticisms, Voltaire, after the example of Virgil once with the Æneid, threw his manuscript into the fire, exclaiming, "Well, then, it is only fit to be thrown into the fire !"

But the president Henault rushed forward and snatched the poem of the *Ligue* away from the flames, not, however, without having burnt his lace cuffs.

In his *King Voltaire*, M. Arsène Houssaye has drawn this sketch of the patriarch of Ferney in morning gown :

"Breakfasting in the morning with coffee and cream, taking no noonday meal, supping at eight with buttered eggs, he worked all day long and reserved but one hour for the strangers who came to pay him their court. The castle board was more abundantly supplied than his own. His hospitality was that of a king. All visitors, all pilgrims, all enthusiasts, found, whatever the hour, a good fowl to besprinkle with wine from Moulin-à-Vent. This hospitality began with the great and did not stop short of the poor. I read in a letter of Madame Suard, that all the peasants who passed through Ferney found there a dinner ready and a 24-cent piece to help them on their way. Would the revilers of king Voltaire, of the *miser Voltaire*, have given *even a pistole?*"

We have already in the course of this work shown how absurd were the accusations of a lack of patriotism against Voltaire. In this connection the letter sent him by Frederick and dated on the 7th of September, 1745, cannot fail to be interesting:

" You tell me so much good of France and of its king," writes the king, " that it would be desirable for all sovereigns to have such subjects, and all republics such citizens. This is really what makes the strength of states, when all its members are animated by a common zeal, and the public interest is that of every idividual."

A volume could be made up of Voltaire's strokes of wit, spirited sallies, and fine repartees, together with the many gems of thought and description coined by him.

He said of Montesquieu: "He restores to human nature the titles she has lost in the greater part of the world."

The first time Voltaire saw Diderot, the latter discoursed almost uninterruptedly and with extreme volubility; he soliloquized with a high-pressure enthusiasm, without leaving his interlocutor the possibility of inserting the slightest remark.

After this meeting, some one asking Voltaire's opinion of Diderot. "Nature has given him a great variety of genius," answered the wit, "but the genius of dialogue has been denied him."

As the penalties inflicted upon those who manufactured false *lettres de cachet* were being commented upon, "It is a very proper thing," said Voltaire, "until the good time coming when those who sign the genuine will be hung."

Excess of work brought quite frequent and serious indispositions upon Voltaire. During his convalescence his amanuensis told him he was drawing too largely upon his health, which was preferable to fame.

"It is not fame for its own sake I desire," replied the master, "for it is only vapor; but I would be surrounded with it in order to be able, with impunity to tell men truths necessary to their happiness."

Another time a young philosopher was astonished at finding him with a Bible in his hands. "I am doing as the counsel in a law suit," said Voltaire; "I am examining the papers of the other side."

Once he exclaimed: "I am tired of hearing it repeated that twelve men were sufficient to establish Christianity. I feel like proving to them that one man is enough to destroy it."

Although fundamentally correct, since Christianity has not recovered, and can never recover, from the heavy blows and keen thrusts he dealt that preposterous system, since his spirit of iconoclasm pervades nearly all forms of independent thought in this present age even, more largely than might be thought, and is found among the members of the church itself, yet he might have amended *this* threat by that other declaration of his, that "all the heads of the hydra cannot be severed at once." But the poisoned arrow—for truth is poison to falsehood—will do its work, slowly as it may be, and the monster, already in the convulsive and maddening throes of death, must, sooner or later, but unavoidably bite the dust and disappear from the earth forever.

In the *Memoirs of Ségur*, is found an anecdote which illustrates Voltaire's pertinacity.

Being at the death-bed of Mme. de Ségur, the mother, asked him to be generous toward his adversaries, since the fanatics were vanquished. "You are in error," answered Voltaire, impetuously, in spite of his 84 years. "The fire smoulders only, it is not extinguished. These fanatics and hypocrites are simply mad dogs; they are muzzled, but they have not lost their teeth. They do not bite any more, it is true, but at the first opportunity, unless their teeth be drawn, you will see whether they will bite or no."

The prince of Ligny has related an anecdote of Voltaire, which is highly characteristic of the poet-philosopher. One day, in his salon at Ferney, J. J. Rousseau was being spoken of. Voltaire, notwithstanding he was still in the midst of a hot polemical contest with Jean Jacques, did not fail to bitterly condemn the decree of Parliament which sentenced Rousseau to arrest. At that very moment a stranger enters the castle yard. He is thought to be Jean Jacques, and some one says to Voltaire:

"I believe he is there now, entering your castle

grounds." "Where is the unfortunate man?" exclaimed Voltaire. "Let him come, my arms are opened to him. Perhaps he has been driven away from Neufchatel and the territory. Go meet him and bring him to me. Everything I have is his."

It is enough to make us say with Jean Jacques himself that Voltaire's first impulse was good. But, notwithstanding Rousseau's prejudice, his later impulses were none the worse for being the result of reflection.

MUNICIPAL COUNCIL OF PARIS.

Sitting of the 11th of May, 1878.

THE CENTENARY OF VOLTAIRE.

The president of the Council reads the following letter addressed him by the Central Committee of the Centenary:

"To the Municipal Councilors of Paris, Citizens:

"On the 30th May *current*, we will celebrate the first centenary of Voltaire, that precursor of the Revolution and apostle of freethought.

"If Voltaire belongs to France, to mankind entire, he belongs especially to Paris.

We, therefore, pray the representatives of the city of Paris to designate the place whereupon the statue of Voltaire shall be erected, and to decide whom they will appoint to lead the cortege of inauguration.

" Accept, citizens of the municipal council, our fraternal salutations.

" For the central committee,

"Signed: GILLET-VITAL."

The council votes unanimously the following proposition of M. Engelhard, proposition covered with thirty-nine signatures:

" Voltaire's statue shall be erected on the *Place du Château d'eau*, on the site of the fountain, which will be suppressed.

" Two fountains shall be built on that same square at the spot where now is the *Marché aux Fleurs* (Flower Market).

" The municipal council will attend the inauguration of Voltaire's statue in a body.

" The citizens are invited to decorate and illumine the front of their houses."